Acclaim for *The Lantern Bearers*

'A subtle and intelligent novel.'
Tom Deveson, *Sunday Times*

'Frame exercises the novelist's prerogative: a privilege that great directors such as Hitchcock can emulate as well as admire.'
Ruth Scurr, *The Times*

'In a novel which makes so many neatly observed contrasts between present and past, the strongest of these is the juxtaposition of Stevensonian optimism with a meanness of spirit which seems purely twentieth-century. The earlier writer would have approved of Frame's generosity towards his characters and of his deliberate avoidance of melo-drama'
Jonathan Keates, *Times Literary Supplement*

'Over the decade 1984–94 Ronald Frame produced five novels and five collections of stories which established him as one of the most impressive young British writers. This confessional novel represents Frame at his best, and, I suspect, marks a crucial stage in the development of his fiction.'
Douglas Gifford, *The Scotsman*

'A master of suspense to rank alongside the greats.'
The Times

'Ronald Frame's excellent new novel, *The Lantern Bearers*, is something of a gem. The deceptive, gentle writing weaves a taut web of insecurity, mistrust, rejection and ultimate revenge. Excellent.'
Simon Lovat, *Gay Times*

Permanent Violet

Ronald Frame

© Ronald Frame, 2002

Polygon
An imprint of Edinburgh University Press Ltd
22 George Square, Edinburgh

Typeset in Linotype Sabon by
Hewer Text Ltd, Edinburgh, and
printed and bound in Great Britain by
Creative Print and Design, Ebbw Vale, Wales

A CIP Record for this book is available
from the British Library

ISBN 0 7486 6321 5 (paperback)

The Publisher acknowledges subsidy from

THE SCOTTISH ARTS COUNCIL

towards the publication of this volume.

Permanent Violet

He has no monument inscribed in stone, no grave shaded by a tree. Instead it's his paintings that bear witness to his life.

A few admirers had started to buy his work when it was first being sold in Edinburgh during the early 1960s. They got into the way of competing with one another whenever each fresh batch appeared.

Colin Brogan's reputation spread by word of mouth. Later, critics and reviewers latched on to the name; they were followed by academics, glad to find a ready new cause.

The Scots have a knack of finding bright talent, and soon tiring of it, and moving on. Colin Brogan has somehow avoided the critical doldrums, perhaps because during his short life he was continually surprising expectations. His work evolved from one style to the next to the next, even though it was using the same subject-matter: his and his wife's domestic life, in several Riviera towns and then at the rented villa in Cassis and the coves roundabout.

Post-War Scottish Painting, catalogue of an exhibition at the Scottish National Gallery of Modern Art, Edinburgh, spring 2002

CHAPTER ONE

Girl with the Flaxen Hair

A sk anyone in Cassis and they will tell you. The artist's widow, the piano teacher, the *écossaise*. In the house with green shutters, hidden away at the end of the lane, 'La Croix du Sud'.

Only now I teach very little. And the paint on the shutters has peeled away in places, to the bleached wood beneath.

Half-Scots and half-French, after nearly forty years of living in France. Somehow I've held on to my Edinburgh New Town ways, even in the broiling summer heat and the mistral winds of the spring. I've retained the illusion of my gentility.

* * *

Back to the beginning of my story.

1958.

Edinburgh.

I'm sixteen and a half.

Now it's my turn to sit for my portrait. My mother has insisted.

'You can't paint Morven and Ailsa and not paint Eilidh,' she tells my father, and she won't be contradicted.

Keep still, Eilidh, can you?
A little further back in the chair, shoulders down, chin up
You can move your head from there to *there*
That'll let you see out of the window, too
But keep your head where it is

And your arms, your hands, that's right
Now try to ignore me
Relax, just be natural
Stay like that, Eilidh
Okay
What's that?
No, I'll tell you know when you can get up
It's easier if I work in silence
Good excuse for *you*, I always tell people: time to do
some thinking
Follow some train of thought, see where it takes you

I feel this is one of our family customs my father would have
been willing to overlook. But his friend Johnnie Melrose,
wearing his agent's hat, was trying to make light of the
business.

'There's no money in it, Ran – not for the moment – but
then I'm not getting my percentage either!'

It was Johnnie Melrose to whom my mother had referred.

'One day they'll be known as *The Three Sisters*, these
paintings,' he persuaded my father. 'When *we*'re all pushing
up daisies. Collectors will be vying with one another to own
all three. Imagine the skulduggery. You owe it to posterity,
Ran – to set up a stushie!'

It's complicated, that word. 'Stushie': 'commotion',
'fuss'. Spoken in Johnnie Melrose's cultured tones, it serves
as a very subtle reminder that although both we Guthries
and the Melroses have ended up living in style only a few
expensive streets apart, the backgrounds of the two families
were originally different.

Johnnie Melrose is an exact contemporary of my father. They
first met at art school, and studied alongside for two years.

My Guthrie grandfather was factor of a big Borders

estate; the Melroses were an old Edinburgh family, well established in the law and banking. The Guthries hob-nobbed with weekend guests to the estate, but had provincial tastes; the Melroses, easy with themselves, had authentically cosmopolitan ways.

Johnnie Melrose decided he wasn't cut out to be an artist, that he was more interested in the business of selling art. He went south, served an apprenticeship in London, then returned to Edinburgh and promptly set himself up in the trade. He rented modestly sized premises at a salubrious address, and was soon assiduously cultivating the right people in New Town and Lothians society. He featured near the top of hostesses' guest-lists. Once he had played rugby, which had resulted in a broken nose; he was left with an imperial profile to those darkly handsome looks.

It was Johnnie Melrose who taught my father about music, theatre, eating well.

Through Melrose family friends, my father was introduced to Lindsey McKinnon. Her father was a Glasgow West End doctor who'd had a fashionable practice before he started drinking too much and misdiagnosing. His middle daughter, my mother-to-be, was never short of helpful friends; she knew to be better informed than anyone else, so that she could hold her own in any conversation, and she was able to add polish where Johnnie Melrose had provided my father with the rudiments of a cultural education. She knew about more esoteric music, baroque opera, and which licensed grocers in Edinburgh had what kind of continental produce on their shelves for the more discerning palate.

Johnnie Melrose was best man at my parents' wedding.

Perhaps weddings were in the air that year, because Johnnie Melrose married six months later himself.

[3]

The Guthries had their first child, Morven. Then their second, Ailsa. Three years after that, I was born and completed the family portfolio.

'That's why I keep working,' my father would tell every new acquaintance. 'Three weddings to pay for.'

Johnnie Melrose still laughed at the remark, as if he was hearing it for the first time.

'I'll know the game's up when *your* paintings don't sell, Ran,' he would quip, as he always quipped.

So long as Edinburgh society needed portraits of itself painted, my father would have his career, and we Guthries would continue to live in clover.

* * *

So, here I am, waiting to be painted by my famous father, Ranald Guthrie, who will one day be knighted.

We're in his studio, which is in a mews lane half a mile from home.

This is where they come, his sitters. Sleek cars drop them off at the door, and they're shown upstairs.

Or sometimes my father goes to them, if they're playing at being too grand, with too little time to spare, and then he paints them 'in situ'.

Whichever, they can be certain they have arrived, so to speak. The more expensive the artist, the more cachet there is in being painted by him: thank you for that early pearl of wisdom, Johnnie Melrose.

Johnnie Melrose is my godfather.

He has fleshed out his role, he wears well-cut, three-piece, tweed suits and jodhpur boots with steel tips. When I was younger he always had a couple of half-crowns for me, shaken out of either jacket sleeve like a magician.

[4]

He used to tell my parents he existed to save me from damnation, and even my mother – with her head full of social duties – smiled at that.

I shall never be like my mother.

You don't acquire her kind of confidence; it's either there to begin with or it isn't.

She knows when she walks into a room just what she can do, what she can get away with. She has an infallible instinct how to dress, whom to speak to, the most expressive angle at which to hold her head.

She knows what she wants. She doesn't put a court-shoe-fitted foot wrong.

In my father's portrait of her she's in two-thirds profile, her head is tilted up to the light, her brow is bathed in it, and her cool eyes shine.

She appears so sure of herself. A quiet and dignified beauty, of an old-fashioned bred-in-the-bone sort: neck stretched long and straight, mouth neither smiling nor unsmiling but patiently, pleasantly waiting for the business of posing to be over; she has other things to do, but she will wait – somehow fixed, established in her own time – while this record is taken, this trophy for our drawing-room wall.

* * *

'Any weekend, so long as it's not Saturday morning. Eilidh can go with you to the studio and you can start on it.'

We've had one false start already, a month ago. This is my second sitting.

We've begun again.

*

Relax, just be natural
Now try to ignore me
Time to do some thinking

If I could only look at my watch
What if I try to tip back my cuff – can I do it?
No. Not really. Damn.

Weekends are out of my father's ordinary run. He likes to stick to conventional office hours, which is the bourgeois in him.

Every weekday evening he will come home at twenty minutes to seven, on the dot, and sometimes there will already be a sour stain of whisky on his breath. He and my mother will exchange a few select details about their respective days. The routine was established when we were children: we would be asked a serious question or two after supper, and then there would be some frivolous banter, and we would get down to more homework or do music practice while our parents ate or got themselves ready to go out for dinner with friends or would-be friends.

La-la-la.
There may be hours of this still to go.
All the time I'm not using today. My conscience aches at the waste.

Rules. Discipline. Self-discipline.
That is the Guthries' way.
Straight back. A tidy appearance. Shoes with a wax shine to see your face in.
We live for others more than for ourselves.
If one member of the family defaults, we are all let down.

Outside, beyond us, presumably chaos reigns. We order the world by ordering ourselves.

> '*First the toe,*
> *And then the heel,*
> *That's the way*
> *To dance a reel.*'

Always one addresses the mirror, to see the person others will see. The mirror is the vital point of reference, the proof. You judge by what, strictly, does not exist.

We live by codes and ceremonies. We prefer understatement and ellipsis to being direct or blunt. We don't put our emotions on display.

Repression and self-control are built into the system; they are part of *you* by osmosis from the moment you're born.

* * *

My father is rubbing out some pencil lines on the canvas. A miscalculation: my face has failed to take shape as he wants it.

Back to the beginning yet again.

I sit thinking of *her*. My mother.

I concentrate. Hard.

How would she be dealing with this situation?

In my father's portrait of her there's a kind of wonder, at what he has achieved: not artistically but socially, by giving this woman his own name.

*

My mother is more poised than I shall ever be. She is more elegant than the other girls' mothers, more soignée than the women my father paints.

She advances on our house-guests, right arm stretched out, offering her long finebred fingers with their strong grip.

Marion Melrose at her husband's side knows the drill, but she has never quite got used to it. She may feel that my father is looking at her with a painterly eye. But she is more likely to be bothered by the physical contrasts with my mother, which anyone can see: she is smaller, squarer, with stubby-fingered hands no amount of manicuring can change. An expensive dress never does what it is supposed to do when it's fitted on her frame and alterations have been decided on.

Husband Johnnie takes her fleshy arm, as if to reassure her. He gets going, into full party mode, and that dispels the memory of any slight awkwardness while his jokes, anecdotes, puns, gossip come tumbling out thick and fast.

'No shop talk now,' my mother will warn Johnnie Melrose and my father. She says she'll separate them if need be, and her voice has a chill edge to it.

She will watch the two of them together, narrowing her eyes every now and then. Marion Melrose is one of her closest women friends, or one of the friends she sees most of, and I wonder if there is a degree of taking her husband on sufferance. She will interrupt a story if she thinks it might be putting my father down in any way, she will dispute him if he sounds too opinionated – but sometimes she will laugh out loud at a Johnnie Melrose joke, louder than anyone else, and then I'm not so sure just what it is she feels.

Afterwards, when they've gone, I will hear her talking about them as if she doesn't quite approve, how they cultivate the so-and-so's and get themselves invited to the parties written up in the newspapers. My father will say, Melroses do a good enough job for *him*, don't they? – and my mother will remind him, Melroses do well enough out of the arrangement for themselves, if you don't mind.

* * *

My father frowns. His eyes dart between me and the canvas. One of us is being uncooperative, the actual Eilidh Guthrie or the pencilled version.

But sorry, Daddy, I'm already on my speeding train of thought. Seeing, just as you said, where it might be taking me.

It's true. Johnnie and Marion Melrose have done just about as well for themselves as the types my father is hired to paint.

A townhouse in Moray Place. Columned rooms, frieze ceilings, a curving staircase that whorls up and up, an oval skylight of stained glass that dribbles its colours down the walls.

At Moray Place my father and Johnnie Melrose will gossip about art matters, and my mother and Marion Melrose about their homes, schools, shops, neighbours.

The Melroses' furniture is inherited, and battered. The paintings are good first-division Colourists, but advocates and surgeons buy the same. My father once painted the family, and there they always are in pride of place above the drawing-room fireplace, at the age they were then, un-changing in time.

We children get on, politely rather than enthusiastically.

The relationship between our fathers might have started as friendship, but now its purpose is also commercial. Who has the upper hand: my father as supplier, or theirs as seller: theirs as agent, or mine as client: Johnnie Melrose as superior tradesman, or Ran Guthrie as the expensive servant of others' glory?

My mother enjoys opera. She has records of Furtwängler's Salzburg Mozart, Erich Kleiber's *Der Rosenkavalier* with Jurinac and Gueden.

Johnnie Melrose was taken to Bayreuth before the War. He knows all the Wagner scores, which impresses my mother and has my father scoffing, all that silly blether about Rhine-maidens and goblins.

Johnnie Melrose also collects records of the Hot Club de France. When he plays them, my mother crosses her legs and taps her feet, she lets the back of the raised shoe hang loose from her heel.

I like the titles and memorise them, even though I can't always distinguish between the melodies. 'R-Vingt Six', 'Japanese Sandman', 'Djangology', 'The Flat-Foot Floogie', 'Blue Lou', 'I'll See You In My Dreams', 'Les Jeux Noirs'.

My mother has a way of relaxing at Moray Place as she doesn't do – not to the same extent – for her other friends, or even in our own home.

She can be Johnnie Melrose's severest critic sometimes, when she is discussing him with my father, but in his own surroundings she quietly teases him, she doesn't humiliate him. Johnnie Melrose is man enough for the challenge, and the two will chide and scold, smilingly done on his part.

* * *

I can hear them from here, from the studio. In my imagination.

Their voices. And the rabble they're up against.

The silence of the studio allows them to fill my head.

Under cover of the party ballyhoo I watch Johnnie Melrose and no one sees me looking, I study those heroic features I know so well, I follow every single movement he makes.

Of all our friends he has the most charisma. It comes from the eyes: sharp and searching eyes, translucently blue around the dark-green pupils, brilliantly blue-mauve.

At thirteen, fourteen years old, I first started surrendering to those eyes.

While I was trying to adjust, to get my bearings, I would find he was making his own assessment of *me*, taking the measure of me up and down.

'Sorry, Ran, there's no money in the Eilidh picture for you. And worse, there's no percentage in it for me!'

My father frowns again.

Don't slump, Eilidh. You're slouching. Back against the back of the chair, please.

I smile at him and pass serenely on.

Where was I?

Johnnie Melrose knows of everyone who might be called a serious buyer of Scottish art: what their tastes and period are, how much money they could be persuaded to spend.

He is a formidable businessman, the undisputed master dealer in Scotland. He is ruthless at getting the price he wants but it will be quite amiably done. He gives you the word of a gentleman, and no one would think to dispute it, seeing him on the rarefied premises of the showroom on Buccleuch Street or in one of his lunch rooms or at his club; his sporting and charity commitments assure you he is a stolidly good type, he has the discreet charm and affable manners of a man who lives with an easy conscience.

For all the demands that are made of him, he also has time to notice my choice of outfit, if my hair has been cut, if I'm wearing something sweet-smelling.

When I know we're going to meet I plan what to put on, I experiment with hairbands and clasps, I sniff at the bottles and tubs of powder on my mother's dressing-table. I take great care to choose differently from last time, so that I will be surprising him.

I've even read up about the Bayreuth Festival, so that if the general conversation should turn that way I will have a decent hand to play; and if the subject is slow in coming, I may be able to chivvy the talk towards it.

* * *

'Saturdays, it doesn't work', my father is telling me. 'Something about Saturdays.'

'Do you want to stop?'

'That's not what I said.'

'But you said about Saturdays –'

'We don't talk in here, Eilidh, remember?'

Passing the dining-room door I heard his name. Johnnie Melrose.

'Well, we don't know, it's just rumour,' my father was saying to my mother when I interrupted them.

My mother turned round and glared at me.

I started to withdraw.

My father ignored me, watching the back of my mother's head instead.

I felt a little riddle knotting the air tight in the room.

Years ago.

I was having my hair cut in the salon where my mother was a regular client. She had left me in the hands of a junior.

'I cut Ishbel's hair too last week.'

'Did you?'

'Gerda, she's due a visit, I'm thinking.'

'Is she?'

'Struan goes to a barber now.'

Why was she telling me about the Melroses?

'But you know all this, don't you?'

I shook my head at the girl in the mirror.

'Your mother always passes it on.'

'Passes what on?'

'What they're up to.'

I watched the girl's eyes, but they were guileless.

'You're all cousins or something, right?'

'No,' I said. 'No, we're not.'

I told my mother afterwards.

'That's absurd. Why on earth should she say that?'

I watched my mother in the windscreen mirror as she drove us both home. Her eyes sharpened to pins. She changed gear too soon; the engine revved.

'The idiot. If she concentrated on what she was doing instead of gossiping –'

My mother's voice was suddenly ragged and angry. I didn't know why she should be bothered.

Yet our hairdressing arrangements were to change shortly after, so the matter was a serious one to her.

Who wanted to be confused by a lowly salon junior with another family? Notwithstanding that each had three

[13]

children of an age, parents who got themselves photo-graphed in *Scottish Tatler* and *Scottish Field*, and a dog apiece – ours an ageing golden retriever and theirs a red setter in its prime.

The Guthries could hold their own with the Melroses.

* * *

'All right, Eilidh, I'm going to go and look for something. Have a break. Get up, walk about. If you'll just remember how you were.'

I stand up.

I stand tall, think of my mother.

When I was a child I liked to put on her hats, her gloves. She gave me an old pair of shoes to skliff about in indoors. I was afraid of the fox's head on the tippet, two gimlet glass eyes which were always watching for me out of the shadows at the back of the wardrobe.

I was continually greedy for knowledge of her, my mother Lindsey Guthrie, and this seemed like a short-cut. It was the closest I could get to the person, the same thrill on my skin which *she* experienced from the clothes, touch for touch.

La-la-la.

I was still a child when I caught someone at a party calling my mother 'Mrs Melrose' by mistake. My mother laughed and laughed. She took Marion Melrose's arm and told *her*, and Marion Melrose picked up my mother's cue and started to laugh along with her.

La-la-la.

That was then, and this is now.

Some uncompleted paintings stand against the walls.

We never discuss our father's work, Morven and Ailsa and I.

Something about those paintings makes me uncomfortable.

Beyond the sense of complementary colours, the careful brush-strokes, I don't get any sense of what my father might be *thinking*.

The sitters have the wherewithal; they hire him, and because it is not in his financial interest to take any risks he gives them what he supposes they want from him: a flattering likeness, with the person depicted against august and plush surroundings.

Everyone is happy.

I stop at the window.

I look across from our New Town to the Old, which is laid out on its barren volcanic rock. The Castle at one end and the Palace of Holyrood at the other.

Where Queen Mary's lover Rizzio was done to death by her enemies, down there in Holyrood, red paint marks the bloody spot on the floorboards.

We all knew the drama from the painting in the National Gallery on Princes Street, Mary with waving arms commands his assailants to spare him while the cornered, splay-limbed Italian prays in vain for his life.

Passion is wild and reckless, and somehow alien to its environment. On the walk uphill to the Castle, the crocodile file from my school would pass cast-iron John Knox on his pedestal, sternly and forever rebuking outside the spiky facade of St Giles's Cathedral.

Where does the truth lie? Somewhere *between* perhaps, about the junction between St Mary's Street and

Blackfriars Street, in a mundane reality spared the violence of extremes.

'I won't keep you, Eilidh.'

My father calls from another room.

He wants this afternoon to be over every bit as much as I do. I shall smell his breath when he returns, to discover if he's had to take Dutch courage: if he's got a Spanish friend, as Johnnie Melrose claims he has himself, the caped figure in fedora who lurks on the label of every bottle of Sandeman's sherry.

'Don't go away now, will you?'

Ha-ha. Not very funny, Daddy.

Saturdays begin early.

My piano lesson is at half past nine in the morning. My mother drives me out to Barnton, to Miss Marjoribanks's trim bungalow with its green roof. She drops me off, and then leaves – with old Ben watching me from his biscuity travelling rug on the back seat – to fill the next couple of hours.

After my solo lesson and the shared theory class I go down to the corner of the main road, looking both ways for a sight of the car. Steering towards the kerb my mother will have more colour in her face, as if the prolonged dog-walking has animated her after a week of housekeeping.

She is always in a good mood on a Saturday morning. Her contentment wears off in the afternoon, until there is sometimes very little left by evening. I consider it *our* shared part of the day; even when my lesson is harder going than usual, I'm glad to have our brief closeness together in the front of the car, just the two of us, and my mother not needing to speak for me to hear her satisfaction.

* * *

My father returns with two photographs of me. He places them on the mantelpiece, where he can turn and consult them.

One dates from last summer. Johnnie Melrose had a new camera, and was looking for some subject material.

I'm aware that a lot has changed since last summer. In another sense nothing has altered. Life goes on as it appears to have gone on for years, but I'm conscious of my body as I never used to be – my body not doing what I want it to, betraying me – and I have feelings which I can't find words for, which I can't even think my way round inside my head.

Also last year.

Johnnie Melrose was crossing George Street. I ran back, so that we would need to pass one another.

I waited for him to spot me first.

'Eilidh!'

What a pleasant surprise this was, how was I, where was I off to?

I told him I was going to look for something for my mother's birthday. He put his hand on my elbow and spun me round, in the direction I'd originally been taking.

'I'm coming with you.'

'Aren't you busy?'

'Not so busy I can't give some time to my god-daughter.'

We went to Jenner's. Ladies' Accessories, the scarves counter, followed by the perfumery.

'Tell me what your mother likes.'

I told him. Which colours, which eau de cologne, which talcs.

He whittled down all the possibilities of choice. This, this, or this. Politely but firmly, he had the assistants stop gabbling at us.

I saw my face in a mirror, bright red. I was hot all over. My eyes gleamed with pleasure, I couldn't check my smile, I was fifteen years old and I was happy beyond words.

He advised me that I select a certain eau de cologne, one that cost more than I had money to pay for. He gave me the difference between what I *could* spend and the total, and wouldn't hear of me paying him back.

'It can be our secret, Eilidh.'

He took me for tea upstairs. He asked for a corner table, and I sat side-on to him doing actressy things, only regretting that I couldn't smoke and so charm him with my Bette Davis arm movements. I saw other people looking, and I wondered what they were thinking as their eyes switched between the two of us. I was hardly aware of the tea or the cake; I was attending only to him and to the impression we were making. I was being an adult, my own person, and I knew as I was experiencing it how it had started, sitting here at our corner table with a pot of Lapsang Souchong and a scattering of pastry crumbs still on my fingers, on my lips.

Something about an exhibition, and 'J.M.' 's part in it. About another Edinburgh artist, called Andrew Mair, who was being written up in the London art press. About 'J.M.' hedging his bets, two-timing.

It was my mother who was complaining. She asked my father, why wasn't he as mad about it as she was? Because, he said, there wasn't anything he could do about it now.

A couple of weeks later Andrew Mair's paintings were with another dealer. My father spoke over our heads at supper; he'd seen the paintings in a window on Hanover Street.

'Really –?'

My mother didn't try to sound surprised.

'Did you know, Lindsey?'
'Marion was saying something yesterday –'

That afternoon Bel Melrose had joined us on the walk back
from school. She was having to help prepare meals while
her mother was away. Mrs Melrose had been gone for ten
days, looking after an aunt, and not much gratitude she was
getting for it.

Had my mother phoned Marion Melrose up in Nairn? Or
had she gone directly to Johnnie Melrose herself, because
she felt so strongly, but didn't want my father to discover?

I wondered if I should drop a hint to my mother, let her
see that I understood her need to be loyal. Several times I
was on the point of doing it, but I finally persuaded myself
she deserved her secret; it was an innocent sort of evasion
and all to a good end.

* * *

Keep very still, can you?
(Here we go again)
A little further back in the chair, shoulders down, chin up
Your head how you had it, please
And arms, hands
Right
Now try to ignore me
Relax, just be natural

Do this, do that

'Tis ever so.

Don't be late, Eilidh. Have you brushed your hair? Is that
cuff clean? Are your shoes polished? Your hem's squint. Oh
yes, it is.

My mother misses nothing.

It's as if she has higher expectations of me than my sisters, she demands more. Even if I am the youngest, there is no risk of my being spoiled, far from it. She forgives Morven and Ailsa for faults she doesn't allow me; I am supposed to have an instinct for avoiding exactly those same faux pas, a sixth sense.

* * *

My father is frowning again.

Yesterday evening I saw him studying the portraits of Morven and Ailsa: as if he was asking himself, why was it easier with them than it is with their sister.

So much is eluding us these days. It has been like this all year.

Finally!

Sixteen years old.

I unwrapped my birthday present from my godfather, from Johnnie Melrose.

It was an LP record.

The first Book of Debussy's *Préludes*. Played by Walter Gieseking.

I asked Miss Marjoribanks if I could try Debussy next.

'Debussy?'

'We haven't done anything of his yet.'

'But why Debussy?'

'Oh . . .' I didn't know what to say. Just because.

'We'll see.'

She wasn't an enthusiast, I could tell.

'If you work hard at the Brahms first . . .'

I did work hard at the Brahms, and Claude Debussy followed in his turn.

It meant finding a new fluidity in my technique, greater suppleness, the grace of not touching ground. I needed to suggest, to evoke, to paint impressions with sound, but not allow myself to be self-indulgent for a moment.

I had to equip myself with a different kind of facility, and yet to make it seem that the playing was quite effortless. I was telling through my fingers something which already existed in the air, a personal reminiscence and also a small legend which belonged outside time.

An enormous geography awaited me, even though the repertoire was modestly sized. Through the ear and in the mind's eye each piece expanded, like a Japanese paper flower dropped into water and which opens and wonderfully blossoms.

Johnnie Melrose was my final judge and arbiter, the person I imagined myself playing for.

I didn't push myself just for my mother's sake, or my family's, or our friends'. I did it for him, so that he would be impressed by me, and think that I had a gift for music which distinguished me from everyone else we knew. I did it really for him, and for myself: so that he would think the very best of me.

'The girl with the flaxen hair,' Johnnie Melrose was saying, and nodding at me.

He placed a piece of sheet music on the shelf of our piano. I picked it up, intrigued.

My mother snatched the pages out of my hand.

'Eilidh doesn't need to have music bought for her. I do that.'

I was shocked. I couldn't look at either of them.

'I heard it played on the radio,' he was explaining. 'And I thought of Eilidh.'

'Well, I've told you.'

'Very plainly too,' he replied. 'I'm impressed.'

'What?'

'A protective mother. Defending her own.'

My mother placed the pages of music at the very bottom of the pile. Everything else weighed down on top of it.

* * *

You're moving, can you keep still?
More still than that
Back against the back of the chair, Eilidh
That's right
Careful with your hands now
And keep your arms how you had them
Relax, will you?

I already have a premonition that this portrait of me will not be judged a success, either by my father or by anyone else. It won't have people's attention drawn to it, as with Morven's and Ailsa's. My mother will prefer to hang it in a dark area of the hall, en route to the kitchen and out of the way.

She's disappointed. She also seems irritated, as if she thinks my father hasn't tried hard enough. He doesn't want it hung downstairs at all, but she insists.

'If the others' are downstairs, then Eilidh's has to be too.'

Whoever's face she has, the girl in the painting, I know it isn't really mine. In the separate features I see only Morven and Ailsa, not the person who confronts me each time I look in a mirror. They take from the Guthries while I feel I've borrowed more from my mother's side of the family, the McKinnons.

There might be some talk of selling the picture. Briefly, it will disappear to the studio; when it returns my father has chalked some marks on the back of the frame. I see Johnnie Melrose looking at it one evening when we have a crowd in. From a distance, then up-close. He says something to my father and shakes his head, then shrugs, which I shall take to mean he doesn't think it's an obvious candidate for the salesroom.

But that is all still to come.

Chin up, that's right
Arms still, please
My father looks past me to the telephone, as if he's willing it to ring and give him an excuse to break off. He wants to call it a day. But we have to persevere, because it's my mother's wish that her youngest daughter should be painted just as her sisters were.

If the phone were to ring –

My mother, enquiring –

Or his old friend Johnnie Melrose –

'Think of posterity, Ran. *The Three Sisters*. Blood on the auction room floor, everyone fighting to get their hands on the three of them.'

I don't care about that. I care about here and now.

I want to be back at the house. I want to have the rest of this Saturday afternoon to myself.

Playing the piano. Playing Debussy, my new passion.

That piece has become the favourite in my repertoire.

When I play it I am the girl with the flaxen hair, and I smile the fact at the bevel-edged mirror on the wall behind the piano. My hair is lighter than either Morven's or Ailsa's;

its colour comes closer to the Melrose children's, and to their father's, bleached from the summer sun and joining his sailing cronies on their boats.

Debussy's music stirs my heart. I contain that inner life. *He* can hear that, Johnnie Melrose, whenever I play to him.

Someone to hear me, to know what it is to care for music. He sits there without interrupting me, and as he listens I feel he is accompanying me beneath the clever surface of the music, into the driving currents. He is sharing the bitter-sweet wisdom with me and the parlous struggle every time – the invalid composer's own diehard exertions – to reach a resolution.

I play for Johnnie Melrose, to show him what the West Wind saw.

In time, when I've practised hard enough, I shall take him with me, not to Fuller's or Jenner's, but to see the hills of Anacapri, to hear the bells through the leaves, to follow my footsteps in the snow, to experience an evening in Granada, its air laden with Iberian sounds and perfumes.

Debussy, which has been *his* choice for me. A private language which we share.

I treat the music as if it is alive, as if it has breath, which means not playing any piece the same way twice. My responses depend on my mood, on the atmospherics, on the time of day.

I shall learn every piece there is, and play each one to perfection.

For his sake. For Johnnie Melrose's express pleasure.

Gardens in the rain, a pond of goldfish. Delphic dancers, fireworks. Moonlight and mist. And, by way of a submerged cathedral, to the island of happiness itself.

*

My stomach tightens, my heart is suddenly up in my throat.

It's crazy, feeling like this: I know it. The blood thrums behind my temples, and I'm having to take shorter and shorter breaths.

My mind isn't in control of my body. I can't predict my behaviour, whether I'm going to make a perfect fool of myself or not.

My skin is clammy, my palms sweat, I have cold perspiration runs under my arms, the insides of my thighs are melting.

CHAPTER TWO

Hourn

W e're off to the mull.
It goes up like a battle-cry at the end of every June.
Another Gathering of the Clans.

We would reach Hourn across water.

The last ten miles or so were a dash, as we raced the ferry coming in up the sound.

On the other side you saw first the line of fir trees in the distance. The serrations became clearer. Some rooftops. A plume of blue-grey smoke from a chimney, or that darker smudgy smoke which a bonfire gives off. More rooftops. The Duguids' saltire flag flapping on its salt-rusted pole.

We would wind down the car windows, catch the smells of the place. Pine, seaweed, mown grass, creosote, petrol from a motorboat engine, that bonfire smoke. The dough rising in the Swiss bakehouse. We would listen out for the rattle of cowbells from behind the bakery door.

Once past the General Stores we had our first glimpse of 'Schiehallion'. Well, at least the old pile was still standing, ha-ha-ha. The Greenland of damp was still there on the gable wall, showing through the grey harling. The wood-work looked as if it could benefit from painting, but it always did, and by now it didn't seem to worsen from one season to the next.

It was one of the most dourly Scottish houses, disdaining frippery. My mother felt that it wasn't really 'us', the Guthries, but it had been the likeliest house available when we needed one. Properties at Hourn rarely came on the market, and we'd had to jump at it, before the reluctant seller had second thoughts and made a private sale to family or friends or – the cold-feet option – rented out through Mrs Minto.

I was seventeen. Another summer, which will be our last there, but none of us could know that.

It was also the summer when I wanted to be different. Different from my friends Peever and Leck and Johnann and Rory B. Until then all that had mattered was that we should be the same. *They* still carried on as before. But I had discovered the need not to be just one of the gang; a voice in my head was wanting to make itself heard, thoughts had to be thought out without others telling me what it was I ought to be thinking. I also had an instinct that I was required now to experiment with my own feelings, and only *I* was going to know how.

* * *

It was a summer custom that my father invited two of his students up to Hourn for a fortnight, for three weeks sometimes if he took to one in particular.

They came here to continue their studies. They painted the land and the sea, or still lifes about the house, or any combination of the human assembly.

Another two presented themselves this August.

One had a supercilious air – as if our haphazard domestic arrangements fell well below par.

The second by contrast seemed quite intimidated by us. His name was Colin Brogan. Behind his back the others called him The Brogan and they hooted at his gaucheness.

*

At mealtimes he would catch my eye. On a signal, a raised eyebrow, I would remind him in mime how to hold his knife and fork, between which fingers, at the proper angle. He watched to see which items of cutlery to use, in which order. He studied how I was eating the crab from its shell, the custard-apple (for someone's birthday) from its skin.

My father called him, sotto voce, 'unsophisticated'. To my mother, searching for a neutral term, he was 'unaffected'. My father told us the young man was ambitious; my mother acknowledged our guest's 'talent'. He didn't really fit into life at 'Schiehallion', but my father had a need to be admired and my mother was quite willing to entertain his disciples when it permitted her to embellish our Hourn existence with a summer salon.

The Brogan unwittingly amused Ailsa with his gaffes of etiquette and his rough accent. Morven preferred to ignore him altogether; she relied on everyone knowing the ground rules, and for that you needed to be '*un intime*'.

I liked the fact that he was physically different. His facial features were bigger, coarser, and he dressed without much thought. I was intrigued by his eyes – brown eyes, intelligent and alert, gentle, sad sometimes, remembering everything.

* * *

The Melrose fivesome were suddenly upon us.

They came every year, to Marion Melrose's sister's house. The Kerrs were childless, and allowed themselves to be swamped by the New Towners. The Melroses, not having the upkeep of a house, could afford to bring hampers of food made up for them by Willis's, and had cases of wine delivered all the way to the door.

Now, as usual, they were all over the place, organising us as if we were unable to do it for ourselves.

[28]

My mother observed the activity coolly. My father said to her, he thought we'd better make an effort.

'Oh, I know how to put on a front.'

'Business is one thing, Lindsey. We leave that behind in Edinburgh.'

It wasn't that straightforward, as they both knew very well. But my father had learned to be diplomatic with his sitters, and I guessed that he missed the full come-and-go with the Melroses since the Andrew Mair dissension.

My mother sighed, theatrically.

'Whatever you say, Ran.'

No, it wasn't as straightforward as that: but we *were* meant to be on holiday, weren't we?

The smarmy student ignored me.

With our other house-guest, the very opposite was true.

I couldn't lose him, he stayed with me. A few steps behind, but it seemed that whenever I turned round there he was.

I fascinated him, although I didn't intend any such thing.

I tried to rationalise the situation to myself.

I was able to talk about music and books and plays, not necessarily from personal experience. I knew quite intimately cities that I had never been to. All learning includes a degree of bluff, of concealing what you don't know. Perhaps he didn't appreciate this, and so he thought I was more intelligent than I really was.

Sometimes what I told him set him off smiling, or laughing.

'What's so funny?'

'You must think this is worth it,' he said.

'Worth what?'

'I don't know. Saving me from my ignorance.'

'Look,' I asked him, 'are you interested or not?'

[29]

'Yes, of course I am.'

'All right. So, where was I, before I was so rudely interrupted . . . ?'

I had something to give, instruction, and what I received back was his readiness to learn.

The sensation was quite new. Nobody had ever depended on me before, not like this.

I may not have understood all the situation's implications, however. Dependence grows sometimes without your realising. And unless you're in time to wean yourself off it, dependence only deepens its addiction.

* * *

His fair skin couldn't take the sun. It fired up, and he was left mapped with livid heat blotches. He knew to cover up, and to stay in the shade. I couldn't see his brown eyes beneath the brim of his hat. I was reminded of my father up on the moors, veiled and gloved against midges like a beekeeper.

I saw Johnnie Melrose talking to them both, Lord Snooty and The Brogan.

Afterwards I asked.

'What was all that about?'

Johnnie Melrose had been telling them how conservative Edinburgh customers were, compared to Glasgow ones. But that he lived in hope of being able to interest more of them in new styles and trends.

'Did he ask to see your work?'

Yes, he'd had a look. But he hadn't offered any very constructive criticism, I gathered: he'd nodded his head, as if he was seeing more or less what he was expecting to see.

It's a start, I said, and I felt I sounded hollow, and that The Brogan didn't deserve *that*.

My father preached the virtues of slowness. Considering long and hard in front of the canvas what you meant to do: blocking in, re-blocking; background washes, multiple layers of washes; the preparation and ordering of the paints.

For my father the art of making art was to perform the business as exactly, as punctiliously and immutably, as some Japanese ritualistic ceremony.

To me that didn't seem the point at all, unless your impressions presented themselves slowly too, unless perhaps the picture was already devised in your head before you began: a fait accompli, which seemed to stifle active thinking and ensured lifeless results from moribund means.

'My favourite god-daughter!'
'I think I'm your only one.'
'You're still my favourite.'
We exchange big smiles.
'So, what sort of holiday are you having, Eilidh?'
'Oh. Fine, thanks.'
'Just "fine"?'
'No. Fine fine.'
I don't know if it is or not, but there is no easy way to respond to a Johnnie Melrose question. I wish I could pirouette and sparkle for him, verbally speaking.

'I always think you're going to hie off somewhere, and leave us to it,' he says.

I'm puzzled by the remark, and unsure how to reply.
'You think I don't fit in?'
'That's an interesting way of putting it.'
Suddenly responsibility for the observation is passed from him to me.

'What *I* say is interesting, you mean?' I ask him.

Johnnie Melrose laughs.

'I think it's what you *don't* say, Eilidh.'

Behind his amiable sherry-party laughter I hear a shrewder and steelier gloss on my character.

My father was an expensive and fashionable artist, and I had to hide my dark secret, of thinking what I thought.

His paintings to me were less confident than mechanical. They would have benefited from some signs of indecision, because then the paint would have been applied differently, with evidence that some nervous energy had been expended. The paint went on too smoothly, too evenly, too inoffensively, too unthinkingly: too *prosaically*, when the sort of painting I responded to was *poetic*.

Poetic art carried all the marks of a struggle of ideas, the contradictory movements of the brush; you didn't ever feel you'd seen a painting for the last time; it attracted you afresh on each occasion, it started its fray all over again.

My father's portraits didn't require your involvement. They were complacent and bombastic because that was what his sitters were, and their 'realism' – the recognisableness of the sitters – was a sign of their having no depth beneath the platitudes of the surface plane. This was who these people were, or thought they were: old money with its pious rectitude, new money with its shiny anonymity.

Of course the paintings might have been exercises in irony, but too little else about my father's behaviour was ironic to lead me to that conclusion.

The more I looked, the more automatic his portraits seemed. People were types, not individuals, and within each group one sitter was effectively interchangeable with any other.

But I couldn't speak of my misdoubts, my dissent. My

[32]

father, because he was in demand and well paid, considered himself a master of his form, and so did others. Johnnie Melrose knew his financial worth, but I hadn't ever heard him express one single opinion on the paintings' artistic merit.

I kept my own opinions under lock and key, double-locked and padlocked.

'You forget nothing, Mr Brogan,' I told him.
'I remember what you said last time, that's all.'
'You commit it to memory, do you?'
'No.'
'But you can quote it back at me.'
'Yes.'
'Verbatim.'
'I'm intrigued, that's all.'
' "Intrigued"?'
'To hear what you think. About art.'
'I don't know anything.'
'You're an artist's daughter.'
'No, no. You misunderstand.'

* * *

All the activity, my mother loved that, the to-ings and fro-ings, people dropping by without an invitation, the never being still, where to next, and do you remember, and Ella Fitzgerald vying with Mozart, planning a meal (a picnic, then, if the weather holds), advising on a wasp sting or how to keep the midges away, running to answer the telephone, listening out for the first ring of a bike bell at the top of the brae, scrambling for a pencil stub to dash down an order for the Stores to deliver, discussing an art show or a concert and then in the next breath reminding whoever's turn it was about helping the girl with clearing away the dishes or about the laundry rota for the coming week, eyeing the condition of paintwork (past your shoulder) or rooftiles (over your head), checking no one had a cup or a plate or a glass that needed filling, comparing the tan on her arms or legs with the others', changing her mind in an instant and spinning round on her ankles so that she turned on a proverbial sixpence, always *always* keeping the room in motion around her, never or almost never letting up, the motor – the dynamo – which powered everything.

There was a piano in the Hourn house; my mother had dug in about that.

I could show off with my playing, and perhaps my mother thought it justified the time and trouble over the years, for both of us. I didn't understand why if she was so proud of my playing she had been so lukewarm about my applying to the Academy of Music in Glasgow.

'The piano is Eilidh's forte,' my father would say, and everyone would obligingly smile, even the Melroses, who had heard him say it more times than anyone else. My mother liked Marion Melrose to listen to me, to prove to her I was in a quite different league from either of the Melrose girls, as I was from Morven and Ailsa.

'I'll be your page-turner.'
'That's a thankless job, Mr Brogan.'
'But you need help with the pages?'
'It's part of the entertainment. Seeing if I can play *and* turn the page. And not send the music flying.'
'If I turned for you, then that would be one problem less, wouldn't it?'
'Oh, solve a problem and there's another in its place.'
'You'd rather I didn't?'

'Have I said that?'
'No.'
'Well, then . . .'

He must have overheard Gillian impersonating his broad Edinburgh accent when she thought he wouldn't notice.

I glared at her, but it was Struan Melrose who caught the glare instead, who tried to smile an apology. The rebuke wasn't meant for him, and I was the one caught off-balance. I found myself returning a smile to Struan, but not so demonstratively.

Further off in time those smiles exchanged between us would become the real damage done.

Apparently I was putting myself down too much.
'Is that so, Mr Brogan?'
'I think so, yes.'
'Well, *you* can paint.'
'And *you* play the piano. You swim. You've read books I've never heard of.'
'They're not gifts of God or something. I just have to practise.'
He shook his head.
'What?' I asked him. 'You think I don't practise?'
'I know you do.'
'I have to be passable at some things.'
Silence.
'Or else,' I added, for something to say.
'Or else what?'
I shrugged. 'Or I end up an old maid, I expect.'
He laughed.
I felt myself frowning.
'I won't be laughing,' I said, 'if it happens to me.'
'Well, it's not going to, is it?'

'You sound very sure of that.'

'Yes, I *am* sure.'

'You can read the future, can you?'

'I wish I could work you out,' he said.

'You can't?'

'No.'

'Work what out?' I asked him.

He didn't reply. But I guessed. He couldn't grasp why I seemed to have so little self-assurance – unless I was just pretending, fishing for compliments.

'The future can look after itself,' I told him.

'Exactly my sentiments, too.'

My father had grown into his Unionism. He had started adult life among the bohemians, the renegades; but for years now he had spent most of his time in the company of the people he painted, both sorts: the genuinely illustrious and the merely self-important. They were mostly Tories, or affected to be, and so my father – chameleon-like – took the colour of the ground on which he found himself.

His students reminded him of the young man *he* used to be. He was affectionately nostalgic and critical with them by turns: wanting to protect them from his scepticism, but unable to defend their political naivety. The world, he knew very well, belongs to the powerful and the rich; it always had, always would do.

Colin Brogan resisted him, charmingly enough. My father saw how receptive he was to his current surroundings at Hourn, and he may have thought these would unsteady him in time, if he was to grow any more familiar with them.

The sophistication. The intellectual ambience. The smell of books in a room. The sounds of music wafting past.

Our guest didn't rise to my father's bait, however. He didn't tell his host that ideas lose their urgency when they're muffled by thick drapes and the bulk of so much furniture. He didn't try to say that art could set about changing the world, that it shouldn't be a vanity mirror for what already exists.

Perhaps my father really wanted to have himself knocked back and told this wasn't how any self-respecting artist ought to live. ('And how is that, Brogan? What is the acceptable mode of existence for an artist? Is it written down on tablets of stone somewhere?')

* * *

I noticed that Struan Melrose was now holding back; he didn't join in the back-chat or the careless laughter which I knew must carry in the students' direction.

I felt that he was wanting me to notice. His eyes were usually trained on me if I turned to look over at him.

I smiled to let him see that I saw, and that I approved.

'Dad said it's not fair.'

' "Not fair"?' I repeated.

'To those two. Sending them up.'

'No,' I said, 'no, it's *not* fair.'

'Can't be much fun for them, when you think about it. Stuck up here.'

'Is it that bad?'

'For them. I don't mean for myself.'

'We should make them welcome.'

'I agree,' he said. 'Sort of.'

' "Sort of"?'

'So long as you don't go forgetting your old friends, Eilidh Guthrie.'

I turned and looked at him. He stood leaning against the wall with ankles crossed and arms folded. Just how his father did, but somehow the son was being more self-conscious. His eyes were trying to hold mine, wanting to see what I read into 'old friends'.

It was an adult expression, and sudden, and I felt that it wasn't appropriate to the place where half my thoughts were remembering earlier summers and where we were meant to relax, *un*complicate ourselves.

The Brogan had been overheard on the phone, enquiring about train times.

'You're not going, are you?' I asked him.

'I'm interrupting your holiday.'

'How d'you know that? Every year we have students.'

'No one's ever left early before?'

'Absolutely not,' I said. 'I forbid it.'

* * *

I took him to the Black Pool.

Clouds were racing overhead. Sunlight and shadows flitted across the placid surface of water. Dark, still water.

He asked why we had come.

'It's a private place,' I said.

'No students?'

Silence.

'I thought it was somewhere new for you.'

'This isn't some kind of test?'

'What?'

'Your father gets you to bring us up here?'

'I haven't brought anyone else here. Dragged them up, against their will.'

'Just joking.'

A longer pause.

'Everyone else sticks to Hourn,' I said. 'The beach.'

'Your father must have painted it.'

'The beach?'

'No, this place. The Black Pool.'

I shook my head.

'No. No, he hasn't.'

I sat down on a rock beside him. I watched him as he worked on the view, over towards the mountains of Skye.

Why oils anyway, I asked him as he was looking for a rag.

Because, he explained patiently, because he wanted to paint seriously. Oil was the professionals' medium, oil was meant for adults.

Or was it, I asked him smiling, was it because my father talked oils and nothing else? (And, I meant, a student didn't dare to go against his teacher's word?)

It seemed to me that the landscape was made for water-colours. The speed with which Atlantic weather changed, the cloud-play, the shimmer of distance, the wateriness of our locale, a kind of *imprecision* we lived with here.

My father wasn't confident at landscape or watercolours. I knew he wouldn't be able to exert an influence with either, except to argue that they weren't worth doing, that an artist proved himself with the human form: a person's physiognomy, he would have said, was challenge enough.

I found unused watercolours in my father's studio, and smuggled them out.

I wanted to give the student a chance to become his own master.

'But if he realises I'm not doing what he wants . . .'

' "*If*".'

'He'd throw me out maybe.'

'So . . . ?'

'And I wouldn't get back in again.'

'He thinks very well of you. Of your work.'

He shrugged.

'You could do your work without him.'

'Hasn't your father got lots he could teach me?'

'I don't know.'

'You'd prefer I just went off on my own and got on with it?'

I felt I was edging closer to a trap, but one that I had helped in setting for myself.

I kept on at him, though.

I told him again, he should try to find his own way of doing things. His own style.

Why should he mimic my father? My father only stuck to his manner of painting because it was a habit with him. An older man has experience, a younger man has curiosity and energy. No, I wasn't being disrespectful, if that was what he was going to accuse me of being –

He tut-tutted at me.

'I wasn't going to accuse you of anything, Eilidh. Why on earth would I want to do that?'

I smiled back brightly, dazzling him – if I had only known – into eternal submission.

He persevered with the watercolours.

He painted quickly, instinctively. He had to think as fast as the paint marks were forming on the paper. He stared at the results.

It was a liberation for him.

I felt I had taken him somewhere new. His work lived for him now as it hadn't done before, it could never again be predictable.

* * *

Some of the others were playing Scrabble one evening.

The word 'BROGAN' appeared on the board.

Then, 'STOOKIE'. (Laughter.) 'FLATFOOT'. (Louder laughter.) 'CRETIN'. (Still louder laughter.)

I was ashamed.

When I got up to go, I noticed Murdo and Catriona exchanging winks. I felt irritated, that I was being seen as this or that. For some reason I felt irritated with Colin Brogan too, because he was causing my irritation to be brought to the fore in this way.

I wanted to lay out my feelings in some kind of straight line, where they would add up and make explicit sense to me.

As ever, I had a white knight to rescue me.

Only Johnnie Melrose, apart from myself, had shown the man some true sympathy.

Following the Scrabble game, he made a special effort. I let him see that I was grateful for his thoughtfulness.

He tried to include our guest in the conversation, he smiled across encouragingly whenever the others' talk got heated or too many names were being dropped, a busy litany of friends, he watched to see that his glass or coffee cup didn't go empty, he would offer him a French cigarette from his case and pass him his lighter.

The two of us, by the broken steps of the terrace.

'Tobacco kills people, Mr Brogan.' I shook my head at him. 'Although they never tell you that in the advertisements.'

'Lots of ways to die.'

'It'd be one less if you didn't. Didn't indulge.'

'Can you be sure?'

'No. But neither can you.'

[41]

'Well, *if* I try to smoke less . . .'
Which was how we left it.

* * *

My mother had a parasol. Japanese, with a bamboo shaft and red-lacquer bamboo ball-handle. An inner circle of cherry-red silk, and an outer round of black. It was quite exquisite, and almost certainly the only Japanese parasol on the mull, or maybe on all the many miles of nibbled Argyllshire coastline.

On the Hourn shore the parasol was raised, and placed on the sand like a wheel, supported on no more than two of its spokes.

Neither quite fully inside nor outside its shade, she enjoyed a very conspicuous kind of privacy.

We're coming back from the beach, the long way round, by Fannish rocks.

Johnnie Melrose holds out his hand for mine, he helps me up even though I might manage by myself.

It's like taking current. For several moments I feel I'm being jolted fully alive by the sensation: the contact of his hand, his skin against my skin, the physical strength he contains.

How would my mother cope with this? I'm wondering. She would have cast him a smile, muttered something, and sailed on. Unperturbed. But I lack her air of unconcern. Insects will bite, I'll stub my toes on the shingle, here and there my suntan is peeling off in white flakes.

My mother is somewhere ahead. But it's me the famous Johnnie Melrose has come to assist.

Briefly for these moments she and I are rivals for his attention.

[42]

I can't believe I've had the good luck unless *she* has wanted me to. But later, when I eventually catch up with her, I can almost imagine that she's annoyed with me. She isn't looking at me. Does she think I've betrayed her?

* * *

I didn't swim in the lochs. Something unnerved me about their opaque, perfectly still depths.

I swam in the sea, in the wild and energising Atlantic, discovering beforehand the rips and tows of currents to avoid.

From the dunes The Brogan would watch me swimming. The water was cold, but I had the bay to myself, it gave me my freedom. The water was aquamarine over clean white sand. The mountains out on Skye were blue and purple.

In the sand, it was said, there was crushed Armada gold, from the galleons wrecked out on the rocks. The evidence glittered beneath me.

He couldn't swim, even doggy-paddle.

I offered to teach him.

He hummed and hawed. Obviously no one had suggested it to him in his life before.

When he tried, he embarrassed himself. That only made me more determined he should see results. To the others he was clumsy and uncoordinated. I wanted to prove them all wrong.

'You've not to let me down now, remember.'

I supported him in the water with my arms; he held my hands.

Anyone could learn to swim, I said, if they kept control of their breathing. The lungs also needed to expand, to hold reserves of breath, and that could only come about with practice and use.

[43]

He seemed to think my explanation was a polite excuse for his ineptitude.

'I'm being serious,' I told him.

'And so am I. I'm never going to be able to swim.'

'You're almost off on your own.'

'Not yet.'

'Don't give up. For my sake, please.'

There, I had said it – and couldn't immediately unsay it.

I was trying to teach him, holding his hands to pull him towards me.

From nowhere Struan Melrose came bounding into the water, spray flying. He offered to give my lesson for me, and he had begun before I could dissuade him.

Struan's way was matey bluster, and letting his pupil fill his head with salt water, so he would know better what *not* to do next time.

It was hopeless. I felt my own efforts were bound to have been wasted now. After this, Struan's hectoring would always be ringing in his ears, the continual dread of being dragged under would defeat him.

He carried on, though, and proved me wrong.

'Just for *your* sake, okay –?'

'Okay,' I said.

In the end he pulled it off. He got from A to B unaided and then muddled his way back to A again. Full of pride for I didn't know whom, for him or me, I whooped in triumph. He lunged at me as if he wanted to hug me, and we both fell into the water, accidentally wrapped in each other's limbs.

Swimming, it's easy to get out of your depth, I said afterwards, celebrating his achievement with some liqueur chocolates I had purloined from my mother's cache of dinner-guest booty. I only realised a few seconds later that my remark also had depths, and it might seem to mean more than I'd strictly intended.

Perhaps he saw my new confusion. I didn't know how to conceal it from him.

* * *

Our Hourn crowd were always rebuilding a bonfire down on the beach. It was lit most evenings. We entertained there, cooked, played rounders in teams, danced to a portable record-player. Sometimes the adults stayed away, and we lay on the sand talking through the twilight until hunger drove us home at last. When dark came early, we would light ourselves through the dunes with a flaming ember.

He had called it 'tribal'.

I heard myself defending our habits.

'I wasn't criticising,' he said.

' "Tribal" isn't derogatory?'

'We started out in tribes. It's in our nature, Eilidh. We'll end up in tribes, the human race.'

'And I'm one of this tribe?'

'Why d'you ask *me*?' he wanted to know.

My mother had a talent for charades. Her only rival at it was Johnnie Melrose. Family honour was at stake while each played hard to be the one who revealed their identity last.

They slipped into their roles quite unself-consciously. My father couldn't forget he was someone having to forgo his dignity, and Marion Melrose, like the other wives, had trouble making you believe she could ever be anyone different from herself.

[45]

In the rising noise of that battle, as we shouted over one another to call out our guesses, my mother and Johnnie Melrose were self-evidently thriving.

Should I go ahead and tell him, We're not who you might think we are, Colin Brogan?

We lived this princely vacation life as if it was our right on earth and not something to be carefully costed, so that it would seem to put us at an advantage over those nouveaux riches who – with their commissions – were actually paying for this performance.

Why couldn't he see? Why had I not let on to him – unless I was included myself in the fiction of the Guthries?

In my father's portraits nobody was real.

His trade was in images. He showed people as they wanted to be seen.

We had lived well on the profits of this fakery; the deceiver was handsomely remunerated for crafting his illusions. But somewhere in the course of our own social ascent, we ourselves had turned into charlatans.

'I might not be who you think I am,' I said.

'How d'you know what I'm thinking?'

'I'm guessing.'

'Guesswork's a bit unreliable, isn't it?'

'Not in this case,' I told him.

'You're not Eilidh Guthrie?'

'Yes. Well, yes and no.'

'Start again. Why d'you say you might not be who I think you are?'

'Because.'

'Because why?' he asked.

'Because I don't want to disappoint you.'

[46]

' "Disappoint" me?'

'Give you a false impression.'

'Is that important to you? What impression of you I –'

'Who said anything about "important"?' I snapped back at him.

It was another custom for my father to drive the students over to the station himself in the estate-car on the last day.

This time, on a whim, I decided to come, too.

I was with them as they waited on the platform.

On my left, that sneery smile which we hadn't managed to wipe off its wearer's face, and some ingratiating remarks of thanks directed at my father.

From my right, a long inscrutable silence.

'Has it been *so* awful?' I asked, lowering my voice. 'I'm sorry.'

He didn't fall for such an easy trick as that.

'You can get back to real life now,' I said.

'What about you?'

'Me?'

'What's real life for you, Eilidh?'

'Well, this is.'

He didn't comment.

I tipped back my cuff and consulted my watch.

'Thanks for coming,' he said.

'To the station, you mean?' I hesitated. 'Oh, I always come.'

Maybe the split-second's delay was all he needed to know, and he would be able to build his hypotheses on that.

He had embarked on the fantasy even before the train pulled in. Standing at the window, he didn't take his eyes off me. I lifted, dropped my shoulders. Steam got between us, a whistle blew. All those clichés.

And my hopes earlier in the summer of being different

[47]

from the others, needing to think out my thoughts separately and apart? I was suddenly irritated with him again, for pointing out to me – even unwittingly – my failed ambitions.

I split my face with a fuzzy-felt smile, an absurd smile, the semi-circular golliwog smile a child draws. Another cliché, and he wouldn't know if it was real or pretend, just as I wasn't sure myself, if this was truly the best I could do or if I was protecting myself with a glaze of satire.

CHAPTER THREE

North British

Back in Edinburgh. My mother was criticising the Melroses about something.

'I wouldn't blame Johnnie,' my father said.

'I'm not *blaming* him.'

'He's good at what he does.'

'Hmmm.'

Had my mother said something directly to the Melroses?

I was with her in Forsyth's department store when Marion
Melrose appeared at the other end of the first-floor gallery.
My mother took a sudden right-hand turn, spinning on those
heels of hers, towards the staircase. Up or down? She started
to descend, telling me over her shoulder that she'd just
remembered an order she had to pick up in Jenner's, pronto.

At Christmas and Hogmanay I didn't have any sightings of
Johnnie Melrose or his wife.

I thought it must take quite a lot of skill for both parties
to manoeuvre past one another so deftly in the middle of the
festive season.

We couldn't avoid the children at the Aeolians' fund-
raiser. There was a dashing white sergeant, and I found
myself partnered with Struan, hands crossed and passing
beneath his upstretched arms and mine. In the Duke of
Perth we met again, and he flung us round with aplomb.

Struan had opted not to try for university, he played rugby,
he and some friends had got up a fine wine society (which

was supposed to be another term for a drinking club), he slept during plays at the theatre, he had excused himself during a Sunday morning service at St John and St James and been seen having a smoke outside.

Even so, I found myself searching to find his good points. He held doors open for women and waited until they were seated first, he had a well-scrubbed look and clean fingernails, his language was toned down for mixed company, he asked you questions about yourself and listened to your replies, he wanted to know which books to read and went out and bought them on your recommendation even if he didn't finish them, he wondered if I thought Debussy was a better composer than Ravel. (I realised *that* information must have come from his father.)

And always his father was there, in the physical resemblance, and in the comparison I was inevitably making: the jejune son against the father, unpolished youth against sophisticated maturity.

Johnnie Melrose was the reason why I always had time for Struan. He was the closest I could get to someone who, I sensed, was unattainable.

'By the way, I meant to say . . .'
My father was looking at me across the dining-table.
'. . . Brogan got the Wardell.'
My mother rolled up her napkin.
'The boy at Hourn?'
'The quiet one,' my father said.
My mother's eyes glanced over at me and away again.
'Remind me what the Wardell is, Ran.'
'The London scholarship.'
My mother nodded, as if she had really known all along.
'Does that mean he's good?' she asked.
'The panel thought so.'

'Oh well.'

My mother got to her feet.

'Another artist unleashed on the world,' she said, smiling wearily past us all.

I had thought about him now and then since my return. But this was Edinburgh and Hourn was Hourn, and to my way of thinking the two didn't directly connect.

He was here in the city, where he had his own friends and I had mine. Several miles apart, we occupied our own separate spheres. If our tracks should cross accidentally, somewhere in the middle – on a busy street like Lothian Road – then so be it. But it hadn't occurred to me to go searching for him.

It turned out he was at the other end of the country. Perhaps I'd only had an instinct all along, that we weren't likely to encounter one another. The experience of London was bound to take him in new directions; he wouldn't be able to guess just where, so how possibly could I?

Ailsa tried to persuade me that Struan Melrose was taking an interest in me. And that it looked as if I was encouraging him.

'Who says?'

'Ma says.'

'And she told you to speak to me?'

Ailsa didn't reply.

My mother hadn't been at the Aeolians' or, the next time, at the Gillespies' for Hogmanay, so how could she know? Ailsa had been at the Aeolians', but not at the Gillespies'.

My mother took up the cause. She said, Struan had never been close enough to us to count really.

'Count for what?'

'Be a confidant.'

'To tell my confidences to?'

'*I* don't know, Eilidh.'

'No, you don't.'

'Please don't speak to me like that.'

'If I *want* to tell him my confidences . . .'

'And Struan Melrose isn't going to tell anyone else?'

I hadn't told him more than I felt courtesy demanded. I had asked *him* questions, about what went on at home. In my mind's eye I followed him back, past the brass name-plate 'Melrose' by the front door and into the rooms of the house in Moray Place.

I was the extractor of confidences, not him.

My mother seemed to resent me having my pleasure. She pretended she was being protective. But she wouldn't give me reasons why she didn't like Struan.

I could have dealt with Struan Melrose by not doing anything in particular, by leaving the situation as it was and so his attention would have moved elsewhere. But THEY – my mother, Ailsa, and Morven by association – forced me to look for opportunities which would let them know I wasn't going to have my behaviour decided by *their* opinions about his suitability.

He had the Melrose charm: less than his father, but ample for those afternoons we spent together. I saw his father's face in certain angles of the light.

He sometimes used expressions I'd heard his father use. He had a lighter voice, but I might have confused them if other voices had also been talking.

His breath was warm on my neck; it gave my skin goosepimples, made my stomach roll into a tight ball.

Whenever I could, I left a space beside me which he could move into. I latched on to the edge of a group in conversation and eased my way in. He and I laughed at one another's punning jokes. We walked in step with everyone else, but kept watch on the other, listened out for one voice in particular.

It wasn't much more than a game. We didn't understand each other any better as a consequence. I didn't feel I went very deeply into myself, to give enough of myself to him. Or that he offered any more to me. It amused me to know I must be irritating my mother, though, *that* gave me great satisfaction.

I was with friends, and their friends. We drifted off in our different directions. Three of us headed back up Scotland Street. Ninian saw Struan Melrose ahead of us, crossing Queen Street; he called out, and Struan waved and sprinted over to join us for the walk home.

Only he and I were left for the last stretch. It started to drizzle, and Struan held his raincoat aloft to shelter us both.

My mother was furious. What had I been thinking of, making an ass of myself like that with Struan Melrose, didn't I have any consideration for my family even if I cared nothing about myself . . .

I couldn't talk to her about it, then or afterwards, so I didn't know if it was my behaviour or (more likely) my choice of Struan Melrose which she so disapproved of. She didn't seem to mind who Morven and Ailsa spent their time with, but *I* wasn't going to be allowed the same licence.

* * *

There must be something in the sombre Scottish stone, in the overcast weather, in the consciousness of living on the damp outer ring of the continent. It all enters into the soul, and darkens it, compresses it. The short summer gone, or in the long anticipation of it, you're left aching for the sun, for some little light in all the greyness.

People's faces are obdurate, undemonstrative: not placid, but fixed-against. There are centuries of behaviour to have to resist, centuries and generations. It's the 'gene' in 'generation' that does you in. How not to become what you are fated to become. In this land of predestination, where you are born to the company of the Elect or the Damned, either/ or and no gainsaying it. It's as if you have to defeat the accumulation of your own heredity, the rigour of your own instincts, before you can even be ready to begin again if you're going to turn yourself into the alternative person who – only you know – is the negation of whatever you are expected to be.

* * *

Struan Melrose guessed I was avoiding him. I tried to hint at the reason why. He kept in touch through his younger sister, who treated the business as seriously as affairs of state.

He wanted to see me again. I gave in eventually, and I was waiting for him out at Corstorphine Hill, at the Zoo. We walked about, not saying much.

We met again, by the Water of Leith. I wondered if he was doing it just to prove something to himself; certainly he hadn't much small talk for me. I was thinking all the time, how different from his father, who was never lost for words. Struan did speak about how boring Edinburgh got and going off to make a killing in the City, and I didn't even know what I was doing with him, except to snatch at details of how the other Melroses lived, any domestic trivia that slipped out, the more trivial and mundane the better.

The second time we weren't so lucky. My mother might not have had the proof, but she could put two and two together; or else I simply wasn't quick enough to deny her when she asked me, I was left flailing around for a defence.

More fury. She wasn't going to tell me again.

'What's wrong with him?'

'What's wrong with *you*, Eilidh? Can't you understand anything I say to you?'

Whatever I do, she's got there before me, she's waiting for me.

I can't think faster than her.

Her eyes bore through me, they drill me to the spot. They've already anticipated all my little evasions.

My guilt couldn't be more obvious if I told her outright.

I can only get away from it when I'm doing my music practice. Two, three hours at a time.

The music is what I have that is mine. My mother can't compete with me there; it's the sole advantage I have over her.

This is my incentive to practice, to establish a small but vital distinction between us. The better I become, the more difficult it will be to slip back and lose ground. I'll have right on my side, and lebensraum around me, so many places in my mind to go.

* * *

In the autumn I went off to the Royal Scottish Academy in Glasgow to continue my music.

My mother tried to have them bunch up my three

[55]

separate lessons for the week, but that wasn't their method.

She suggested to me, I'd probably prefer to make my own way there. I thought it had to do with not embarrassing me in front of others, dropping me off and picking me up in the car. And then I realised it was bound to take up a good deal more of her time, and why should I expect it?

I travelled the forty-five miles there and forty-five back on the train, and for the first two or three weeks – in an Indian summer – I seemed to be making the journey in brilliant sunlight, in a boiling compartment.

My head was filled with fantasies of a life for myself, always concerning music and my inordinate talents. I turned and watched my reflection in the window glass, seeing whomever I wanted to see there. An international concert pianist, a recording star, or the doyenne of music teachers, or a New Town hostess who silenced guests with the fire of her playing, or a famous composer journeying south – to sun and heat – for inspiration.

My life lay tantalisingly open before me.

A myriad possibilities, so many that the breath seemed to get battened down in my chest as I thought of them, I was left having to take gulps of air, swallowing them hard, and then needing to lean forward to cough.

The future shimmered, it shone, on and on.

The postman delivered to Royal Circus early, so even though the mornings were a rush I could take mail with me to read on the train.

My mother was at the door before me one morning, picking up what had fallen through the letterbox and sorting through it. I noticed her slip a postcard below several letters in her hand. An Old Master landscape.

'And these are mine. Nothing for you today, Eilidh.'

Her little pile was left on top of the sideboard. I lifted it up, to find the postcard. A Watteau. *Les Deux Cousines.*

I turned the card over. It was addressed to me. Addressed very legibly.

A whole year in London! They work you hard – it's a fair slog – but I make the most of my free time. Went to a Debussy recital, so maybe I'm not a lost cause entirely. Digs in Lamb's Conduit St – name is best thing about it, but I'm more out of the place than in. Hope this finds you as it leaves me. Colin B.

I put the card into my pocket, and ran for the front door.

On the train I looked closer at the picture. A young woman was being serenaded by her suitor playing a lute. Her cousin was standing a little distance apart and with her back turned, facing the view of misty park in front of her; she was unwanted by the other two, who were rapt by one another, and she stared across at a statue on a plinth, which might have been her own frozen reflection.

When I got back, in the evening, the removal of the postcard wasn't mentioned. I had supposed my mother must have failed to see it was addressed to me. Yet I thought it was curious that she was taking great care not to look at me, or not to meet my eyes, and I wondered why in that case innocence should be so diligent.

* * *

Another day. I was on the train heading west, searching through the contents of my music bag. When I looked up, Struan Melrose was sitting on the other side of the compartment, in the seat opposite mine.

I felt the colour rise to my face, blaze across my chest. It was the only answer I was being requested to give him.

[57]

He told me he had some work to do for the firm of Edinburgh stockbrokers he was apprenticed to. We discussed that for a while, until he turned the conversation back on to me and asked about my musical studies. He told me he was very ignorant about classical composers, and I was suddenly grateful to him for his honesty.

In Glasgow he walked me from the station.

Would I care to have lunch with him?

I hesitated.

He wasn't in Glasgow very often, he said, it would make the day even more special for him. If I were to grant him the pleasure of my company –

He sounded again like his father's son. How could I have resisted that masterly, surefire Melrose charm?

I discovered that lunch wasn't to be a simple business. He had booked a table for us at Rogano's.

' "Rogano's" ' I repeated.

He laughed.

'D'you know what it costs there?' I asked him.

'It's *my* money. I've earned it.'

We stepped inside from Royal Exchange Square, into the coral-glow and Art Deco splendour. Black marble, silver vitrolite, up-lit bas-relief sea murals, dazzling white linen.

Two sherries each for aperitifs, and already I was beginning to feel woozy.

Lobster thermidor, because he thought that we should.

French wine. A Loire Muscadet. Before I knew it we were on to a second bottle.

He was getting to seem less and less like his father. He spoke about him only when I enquired, stumbling over my words. I felt I was nearly as well acquainted with the man as he was.

'You don't want to hear, Eilidh.'

[58]

'Yes, I do.'

'I don't see why.'

'Then you don't know me,' I said.

'We don't want a ghost at our feast.'

'I don't have a problem with spirits.'

'Then drink up!'

Ghosts wouldn't have been out of place. By now I felt suitably light-headed and receptive.

I shook my head at him. Not understanding was only confirmation after all of how unlike his father the son really was.

He nodded over at a champagne bottle in a bucket. He told me a champagne cork should be drawn from the bottle s-l-o-w-l-y, the French way.

' "The French way"?' I repeated.

'Softly. So I read once. "No louder than an erotic sigh".'

I heard myself starting to laugh.

'Is that so?' I said.

I laughed and laughed, and couldn't stop.

When we left the restaurant I tripped on the step. He gripped my arm and led me across Exchange Square. This wasn't the way to Buchanan Street. But he told me I needed to rest, and for that purpose – I was laughing all over again at his neat logic – he had taken a room at a hotel.

'A hotel? Which one?'

'N.B.'

'The North British?'

Very smart place, I started telling him, British Railways give them some style, don't they, my Aunt Ro had her wedding reception there, when she got married, I forget what her husband was, I mean *is*, a lawyer, barrister, or the other one, a thingummybob –

I don't remember how we got there, by cobbled lanes and

back ways. He knew to use a side-door of the hotel and ushered me inside. Upstairs by the lift, while he made conversation with the bellboy to deflect him from my sorry state.

He unlocked a door. I stood outside in the corridor, vaguely resisting, until he circled my waist with his arm and gently directed me forwards.

There was a large bed for me to rest on. I started to say something about it, but the long words came out slurred, in quite the wrong order, no use at all. He took away his arm, and I had to reach out, grabbing his shoulder.

He steered me towards the bed. A double bed.

I dropped down on to the edge of the mattress.

The room tilted, it seemed to be running away from me. I covered my face with my hands.

He undressed me carefully. Every item of clothing I was wearing. He laid me down on the white sheets.

When he came back he was naked. With the light behind him and his face unclear, I was confused for several seconds, just who . . . When he leaned forward, I didn't recognise whose soft voice this was, such delicate words being breathed over me.

Maybe once or twice, fleetingly, I did try to resist him. But he showed me that it was pointless, smoothing my hair, caressing my limbs, kissing me on all the private places of my body. Nothing was sacred any longer, moment by moment I was being taken further from the person I had been and there was no way to get back.

Afterwards I lay saying nothing. What could I have said?

The room had a bathroom, and he had pushed the door almost shut while he showered.

I had walked, lurched, staggered into this trap, and no one to blame but myself, no one. I watched reflections from

[60]

the street pass across the ceiling. I felt I was looking up through water to the glittering, inaccessible surface. I looked up through a terrible calm, every sense in me dulled, a deathly stillness was holding me.

* * *

For the next few days I was bewildered. I was angry. I was ashamed. I was completely at a loss to know what to do.

At least he had protected himself: for his benefit, I supposed, rather than mine.

That excused nothing, but at least I knew I couldn't be carrying his child.

It was the sole reason to be relieved about anything. Not to be totally in despair.

Damaged goods. But there wouldn't be any immediate 'consequences'.

Never mind that my brain was in freefall. There wouldn't have to be an operation. I could keep up a pretence for a while, maybe.

I waited for a phone call or a letter.

The days dragged.

At intervals I would be shanghai'd in my thoughts back into that hotel room, I was seeing his face above mine. I had the heat of his breath on my neck; he was opening me up with his fingers, he was whispering to me his soft, sweet obscenities.

But not a mention of love.

I felt lethargic and heavy: drained, washed out. As if I was looking out at the world from far away, from my quarantine of shame. I didn't know what the signs of guilt were, but I must have been showing them. I trained my eyes away from everyone else's, kept myself bundled up inside. If I thought I was going to cry in the street, I looked up to Glasgow's high sandstone facades, to the statuary there, an alternative world where no one wept, lolling giants, nymphs and naiads, a few goddesses, warriors and amazons, and the whole grand bestiary of lions, horses, griffins, unicorns, a couple of stags with hewn antlers, 14-point imperials.

I was terrified now that he would call or write. What could I say to him?

He had taken what I would never have restored to me. But what had I got back from him?

I looked in the mirror to detect any differences there might be. Slowly, surely, they appeared. A defensive hunch of the shoulders – a furtive unwillingness about the eyes – a new straightness to the mouth – tension in the wrists and hands, like wires pulled very taut. I eyed these latest developments dispassionately, and *she* reached out and touched the cold screen of mirror glass between us.

My mother made no comment. But she had a way of probing me with her eyes, stripping back my concealments – what I was saying, doing – and again she was pinning me to the wall, like a specimen for dissection.

She waited for me to twist my head away. It was cruel, but it was the bond between us, that she could be so critical and that somehow I deserved this treatment.

'I've got things to do,' she would say, and leave the house, casting a little perfume trail behind her. Out on the pavement her limbs loosened and she seemed relieved to be gone, as she strode quickly up the hill in her off-to-town clothes without a backward look.

But I had been as guilty as him.

It had needed me to be there *for the thing to happen*. I had gone with him, more or less of my own accord, *and the thing had taken place*.

For some reason, *why why why*, my brain was screaming at me not to be unfair to him.

* * *

When we met at last I had no warning.

He was in the back of a car of smiling faces that drew up alongside. I smiled crazily back at them, found myself talking with no prior knowledge of what I would say, tugging at the string of beads round my throat.

He was leaning forward, looking up at me. I wanted to pummel him with my fists, burst into tears, shout back obscenities of my own, go running off. But I stood at the kerb, continuing to talk, intermittently meeting his eyes while Calum and Andrina chattered over one another and laughed.

He didn't open his mouth except to smile, and it was only *him* I wanted to hear, his voice. I hated myself for caring, for giving him a second chance, and all the time I was seeing myself standing on the kerb talking, as if I was someone else observing, just a chance passer-by.

Walking away, I was shaking all over, unable to help myself.

I heard the others' laughter in my head, from summers long ago.

I felt I had lost my childhood too; it had been filleted out of me, skewered out with a hook.

I kept leaking between my legs. The spoiling had been done. I bathed in the hottest water I could bear. The bathroom

[63]

would grow so steamy that the paper on the walls where the tiles stopped peeled away here and there, along the seams, and I had to glue it back down.

Back to the piano.

Swathes of sound. Church bells across the valley. Gardens under rain. The drowned cathedral.

I dropped down into the depths of the music. Layer beneath layer beneath layer, fathoms down and down.

* * *

On the train. Where else?

It was bound to happen finally.

We found standing space at the end of a corridor. I couldn't look at him.

He apologised. For the silence, for not having got in touch. He'd thought we needed time to think about matters, each of us.

I shook my head.

'No?'

I shook my head again.

He stood shuffling his feet.

'I don't think there's anything to say,' I told him, and my voice stayed strong.

'Eilidh –'

I pulled my arm away.

'– please, Eilidh.'

I knew now, although I hadn't known only five minutes ago. There wasn't anything to think over, there was nothing left which needed saying.

I realised someone was following me round Melvin's music shop by the bridge.

I saw a man's shape out of the corner of my eye.

I turned away, I was about to make a bolt for the door.

'There's *nothing* here you want to play?'

I stopped, spun round at the voice.

Johnnie Melrose.

I felt my control go, the shakes came back, my eyes filled with tears.

'What on earth's the matter, Eilidh?'

How could I possibly tell him that?

All the past weeks were breaking over me.

He had his arm round my shoulders; I fell against him. I desperately needed his comfort. I couldn't hide that from him. I had no defences now.

In the background a record played over the sound system. A jaunty concerto, trumpet blaring triumphantly.

His hand on my back. The strength in his upper arms, his shoulders. The scratch of his five o'clock shadow on my brow.

'Come on,' he said. 'Let's go out and have tea somewhere.'

Fuller's, the inner sanctum. Among the hats, the silk turbans and velvet berets. A quieter table at the back.

In the Ladies' Room I made myself look more presentable. I would do anything now not to embarrass him. I returned wearing a shrill smile.

I couldn't remember afterwards what we talked about. I only remembered sitting thinking, here I am sitting with him again at last, with this man whom the other women in the room are turning their heads to look at, who is served with special attention by the waitresses, this man to whom everyone is drawn. Nature has her favourites, the stars shine down on some, and I feel lighter in my body and spirit for being with you.

How could it be that he was the father of that son? It made no sense to me at all. A travesty of nature. The father couldn't excuse the sins of the son, but he could grant me solace, which was like day to the other's night.

My mother was looking at me curiously when she got home.

Had she heard somehow?

It wasn't any of her business, not now.

And heard *what*? About tears in Melvin's music shop, in full view of the other customers? And why should I have been grinning like a country daftie, until my stretched mouth hurt, among the Fuller's sobersides?

* * *

Another criticism of the Melroses. It was from my father this time, that they hadn't replied to say if they'd be coming to an 'At Home'.

'I didn't invite them,' my mother said.

'You didn't invite them?'

'There's an echo in this room.'

'Did you forget?'

'No, I didn't forget.'

'So, why . . . ?'

Because, my mother said, she had reason to believe that they didn't get on with the Carswells. Marion Melrose didn't see eye-to-eye with Elspeth Carswell.

'Why not leave the Carswells off?'

'They haven't been here before.'

'Why have them at all?'

'Because, Ran, *you* wanted me to ask them.'

Which was as far as the matter went. The Melroses

weren't expected. My father withdrew from the argument, and my mother didn't express any regrets.

* * *

I had been as guilty as Struan Melrose.

It had needed me to be there with him *for the thing to happen*. I had gone with him, more or less of my own accord, *and the thing had taken place*.

CHAPTER FOUR

The Stobo Road

A telephone call just before midnight. Only bad news travels so late, but none of us could have guessed, not really, just how bad.

Moonlight. Then the beams of torches, tracking across a field, locating the debris of a car.

Voices. Men are shouting. Get help!

It's too late for the car's passenger, the woman.

The male driver is still breathing, with great difficulty. There's some hope for him at least. But *she*'s like a mangled doll, a folded puppet without strings.

My mother will always be riding in that car driven by Johnnie Melrose.

The facts.

Lindsey Guthrie was a passenger in a car travelling on a country road near Peebles, between Broughton and Stobo. The car, an Alvis, at some point left the road and rolled downhill. The car ended up a wreck, with my mother dead inside it.

Two farmhands said they had seen a sports car speeding past, driving too fast for the concealed bends up and coming.

The police concluded that the car slewed into a tight corner, swung round, cleared a low wall, and then started careening downhill. It somersaulted at least twice, and landed upside down. On final impact the roof struts crumpled and projected into the cabin space. One broken spar of metal pierced my mother's chest, puncturing her heart. She must have died instantly.

There had been a recent shower of rain, and the red tarmacadam of the road was wet: only lightly wet, but that would have been hazardous enough if the car's speed exceeded 50 mph, making for an unseen corner.

The police recovered some belongings from the field.

My mother's alligator handbag, with its efficient clasp still neatly closed. Her shoes, which she must have taken off. A red and black silk parasol, with its bamboo shaft snapped.

An empty champagne bottle had somehow survived intact.

Some days later a shepherd found a powder compact, with its mirror cracked, which my mother had probably been using at the time when the car lost its grip on the road. Nearby was an open tube of lipstick.

Only Morven could bear to view the body before our mother was buried.

The terrible thing, Morven said, was this: she was faintly smiling as lay there in her Jean Allen dress, with her face made up as if for a party.

Smiling. A Mona Lisa smile.

As if she was going on ahead, I thought, as if she was going to get things going at her party. Later he would show up, the only guest she was waiting to welcome. The evening would come alive, if that was the term: now that *he* was here. The evening was only the preliminary for the long, long night ahead.

*

Johnnie Melrose was in intensive care in an Edinburgh hospital.

None of the Melroses came to our funeral. Their wreath of white and yellow lilies was returned.

Morven only told me that our father wanted it this way.

But why is my father not grieving as I am?

I would know if he was trawling infernal depths. If a Greek tragedy was being enacted inside him, I would hear its echoes. I should be seeing his wretchedness, I should be despairing at the sight and sound of *his* despair.

He looks at me quite dry-eyed, however, and his mouth is set straight. As if to tell me I'm monopolising grief, which is not my right. But I'm jealous of what I feel, I'm possessive of this troubled sorrow which I can't explain to myself. I won't give it up, even for cold looks and the disapproval of the person who thinks he's the only one entitled to give it.

Something I overheard Morven saying to Ailsa.

'Who knows *how* long it was going on for –?'

Morven can speak to Ailsa as she would never speak to me. Ailsa is closer to her in age, but it has always been this way, an instinct to confide in Ailsa instead of me.

I'm younger, yes, but, more than that, I'm different.

I look more like my mother than either Morven or Ailsa. My father sees the resemblance, it confuses him. He's moved, and he's gentle to me; but at other times he doesn't stop finding fault, I can't please him, the mere sight of me exasperates him, and all that matters to me then is to get away.

I stand outside rooms, door open, and I have to dare myself to go forward. I'm expecting to see a blur of move-

[70]

ment, my mother's, or hear her footsteps fading, not quite out of earshot.

The worst of it is, thinking that she died when she was happy: speeding along the Stobo road late one afternoon, happier with him than she could be with us.

Her clothes still hung in the wardrobe.

My father had changed bedrooms, rather than have to deal with sorting out her belongings.

I could still smell her on the clothes. Her talcum, so that I was inhaling the presence of her living body. Here and there a fallen hair from her head had twisted itself into the fabric; I uncoiled it, held it in the palm of my shaking hand.

A car goes rolling downhill. It gouges wheelmarks into the soft grass. It rolls over once, twice. Metalwork buckles, the chassis severs, the windows fall out in a harmless-sounding trickle of tinkling glass.

* * *

There was so much to do, just to keep everything the way that it was.

My mother had known the secrets of how the house was run. None of us could do it alone, and when everyone tried we just ended up getting in each other's way.

Meals. Laundry. Cleaning. Repairs.

All we were trying to do was re-create normality. We had been so used to it, we couldn't think how it had been done.

If we could only have asked my mother . . .

The Guthries had nothing more to do with the Melroses.

I wanted to see what signs of sorrow my recuperating

godfather showed, how the tragedy had marked him. His eyes would tell me, if I looked into his eyes, long enough to see what he wasn't admitting to: black pools of grief, where he must suffer alone.

But people spoke of him being much like his old self. He wouldn't be drawn into talking about certain matters, otherwise he was affability itself.

I didn't know how they could be correct, unless he was putting on a masterly show for them, *playing* at being sociable. How could he possibly continue to get up every day and attempt to live his life just as before, how it once used to be?

The Guthries muddled on, as best they could, while the Melroses kept up a front of their own.

Meantime my mother passed into the eternal vacuum of history.

Officially we had nothing more to do with the Melroses.

But inevitably there were occasions for (almost) meeting: for spotting one another in the distance and attempting to take evasive action. Now and then there would be an unavoidable encounter on the turn of a staircase or on a narrow stretch of pavement.

We coped however we could, with wide-open eyes and instantly tight, squeezed-out, meaningless smiles which we wouldn't have attempted if we'd had a couple of seconds to think about it.

There was nothing to talk about. Which really meant, of course, that there was far too much left to discuss, but where in God's name to begin.

She died without us. She died with *him*. That was just how she would have wanted it: not the truth becoming public knowledge, but to be with the person she truly loved. So long as they were together, the consequences must look after themselves, even this social trauma. Who'd had to give up the most, after all?

'A quick death's best.'
'She didn't have to suffer.'
All the platitudes we were offered.
Perhaps my mother *had* deserved to suffer, if all were fair. She tried to steal happiness for herself, however she could, and she was quite shameless about it. She simply supposed we wouldn't get to find out.
Catch as catch can.

When I have the house to myself, I put on her things.
The famous Hartnell jacket. A Herbert Johnson hat. A pair of mauve suede gloves.
Her shoes are a size too small for me, but I prise my heels in with the help of a shoehorn.
I walk towards myself in the mirrors, or retreat, swivel on my heels, walk away until I have to turn, and then I start again, walking towards myself in the mirrors.
I sit on the chair, by the dressing-table. I cross my legs, trying to remember which way, left over right or right over left, and needing to reverse for the mirror; everything has to be referred to the glass.

I smell her; she is still here. I'm no match for her, and she always knew that. The clothes don't make the woman, and I have to take them off despondently, defeated to the end and beyond.

* * *

My father had no alternative to changing his dealer.

Work was all that kept him going, so a new arrangement needed to be hit upon quickly. He switched to Melrose's rivals, Rutherford McGavigan, and to the senior partner, Forbes Rutherford; he'd had an impressive career, but his glory days were behind him, when he used to cut and thrust with the best of them down in London.

One day I lifted the lid of the piano and played a few chords. They sounded out of tune.

It was like a verdict.

I couldn't play after that.

The music contained a stupendous, terrible betrayal.

Buried at our feet, with her name on a headstone (Guthrie née McKinnon), my mother seems to belong more than ever to herself. Polished black marble; the hard, unyielding frosted earth; in the urn, vividly yellow daffodils surviving the cold with hosannah-ing trumpets.

She draws me back. I could start to forget, if she wasn't here, in this place which – when I'm somewhere else – I'm always aware is where I am not.

Safe now.

In the past tense she was free of us. She wouldn't age, she wouldn't have to deal with the indignities that come to women as they grow older. She was an amalgam of all the younger selves she had been.

Finally she would be with Johnnie Melrose, travelling with him in the Alvis forever, on that unending red road which winds along the hillside of sheep pasture between Broughton and Stobo.

*

And yet . . .

And yet everything in the past becomes suspect. Everything is capable of reinterpretation. No memory can be relied on.

The mirror of the past is now a refracting prism.

The mind can't concentrate, can't settle.

That is the worst legacy of all.

I was playing one of her records. I was smoking one of her cigarettes. I was wearing one of her suits – the jade Jaeger boiled-wool – her best Givenchy perfume, her South Sea pearls.

I turned round.

My father was back. Standing in the doorway. He should have been in Glasgow for the day.

He came across. He knocked the cigarette out of my mouth, so hard that he cut my lip. With both hands he grabbed the strings of pearls and snapped them, the pearls went flying and scattered on the floor. He hurled himself at the radiogram and sent the needle slithering across the record.

'Get those clothes off before I tear them off you.'

Terrified I peeled the jacket and skirt off in front of him. I couldn't see for tears. I started to sob.

He told me to get out, he didn't want me in the house. Just stay away.

'What?'

'You heard me.'

'Stay where?'

He shook his head.

'Stay away till when –?'

'Till I tell you.'

The door slammed behind him.

I stood still, I couldn't move. I was turned to stone.

I repelled everything. Standing there in my mother's underskirt, nothing reached me, nothing could get through. I felt as remote as the sky, I was as cold as heaven.

Morven came to the Gillespies' – and fetched me, took me home.

'He wasn't thinking what he was saying, Eilidh. It won't happen again.'

How could she know that?

'Daddy just forgot. Everything's been so ghastly. It'll get better.'

* * *

Johnnie Melrose still wouldn't speak about the accident. Not a word to anyone.

He had retained his partnership in Melrose's, but others now presented a public face for the firm. He might still put in an appearance at one of the charity functions he used to frequent, but only briefly, as his wife requested. The great pavement-strider had taken to riding in taxi cabs, which we had always thought rather vulgar, but they sped him hither and thither with a modicum of privacy. He stopped lunching at the Pompadour and defected to the Café Royal, a table against the wall in the second room, where he was difficult to distinguish among the shadows.

Marion Melrose remained Mrs Melrose. Several stories did the rounds that she was going to take off and live somewhere else, away fom the watching eyes and wee censorious mouths, but it didn't happen. In the New Town you knuckled down, drew your lizard-skin belt tight, and got on with it.

* * *

I copied out my mother's signature, over and over until I couldn't tell the difference between the original and what I had just written. I imagined that this was *her* writing hand at the end of my arm.

I haunted the places where we used to go.

I went back to find us, my mother and myself, *as we were before*. Maybe there would be some way of undoing the accident, so that it didn't happen, and there was no need for her to go to Stobo as she did that day.

I had read that it's possible to cure some illnesses by walking a very long distance. Over days, weeks, however long, you walk your sickness out. But sometimes it works for someone else, you walk *to* them, many miles, scores, hundreds, you take on the burden of their malady and wear it down.

I was trying to walk out my unhappiness. I was also walking for my mother's sake, in order to cure whatever deep dissatisfaction it was with her life that had led to her death.

I wore through the soles of my shoes, endlessly walking.

I wrote out lists, long lists. I felt that if things could be written down and listed, then they had an authenticity, and I'd hold on to them.

The plays and concerts we saw, the characters from books we used to speak about, all my mother's wearing outfits, the birthday and Christmas presents she'd given me and I her, the dishes she cooked for us, everyone who had ever come up to Hourn to visit in summer.

I went into churches. An organ might be playing, and I would sit at the back. A cleaner clattered her slop bucket, or a helper banged the dust from bibles. If I chalked up enough appearances, maybe – God willing – I would be due my own miracle.

* * *

Five months after the funeral Morven was married to her advocate admirer and ensconced in Ainslie Place as the second Mrs Lorimer. Alasdair's friends were suddenly her friends, and older than herself, but she had accounts with all the best shops in Edinburgh and was being welcomed on to charity boards, no experience necessary.

Ailsa was going out with someone she'd first met when they were six years old. She was easy with his medical set, and she cheered from the sidelines on Saturday afternoons when his team kicked the ball into touch, and she kept busy turning the two of them into a bona fide couple, a social partnership.

I was filled with the same envy and disdain for both my sisters.

We three divided up our mother's jewellery.

Morven said she wanted only one small keepsake. I heard her telling Ailsa when she thought I was out of the room that she didn't want to wear things which had brought such bad luck in their trail.

So, Ailsa and I split up the spoils between us. Ailsa managed to lay claim to the simplest settings, while I found myself with the older, heavier items. But when I enquired at a jeweller's afterwards I learned that the stones were better in these inherited pieces than in what my mother had bought herself. I didn't tell Ailsa, and considered it a just desert.

A car goes rolling downhill, ripping up the green turf of the field. It veers wildly, zig-zagging. It leaves the ground, somersaults, smashes down on to its roof once, twice.

The bodiwork buckles, the chassis severs, the windows fall out and the glass fragments lie glittering like diamonds as twilight comes on.

* * *

My father's career didn't ever again reach the heights it had done with Johnnie Melrose. He must have realised this, and had to suffer the knowledge in silence, without my mother there to discuss the matter with. He was ready now to err on the side of blatant flattery: narrowing his sitters, lengthening bourgeois legs so they had the proportions of aristocratic shanks, making workaday hands look finer, softening facial defects, restoring lustre and volume to dull and thinning stressed hair.

Johnnie Melrose had once or twice cursed the hagiographer in my father, using alcohol and humour to make his point. Teetotal Mr Rutherford with his stretched mandarin face didn't judge it worthwhile commenting, and left the goose to carry on laying golden eggs. But the gold was bit by bit becoming debased, losing the high value it had once held in the trade.

Someone said they'd seen me hanging about outside Melrose's showroom.

I told my father, 'It's none of their business.'

'They were only trying to be helpful, Eilidh.'

'How do they know anyway?'

'Can you tell me that it *wasn't* you?'

'You'll have to ask a philosopher that.'

'Don't try to be clever with me, d'you hear. For Christ's sake!'

Why is my father so angry? He's being King Lear. Morven and Ailsa stand in his shadow, and I'm Cordelia now. A tragedy is playing itself out.

*

Again, but this time closer to the Melroses' home in Moray Place.

I told my father, 'I can walk where I like surely.'

'You're not walking anywhere.'

'Who says that?'

'*I* say.'

'I'm not a child.'

The word 'child' was like a goad to him.

He spat out his reply.

'If you hadn't been born . . .'

What was he saying? I couldn't answer him, I didn't have breath in me, my chest hurt.

'Your mother didn't need to have you. But she did.'

My blood ran cold. I turned to ice.

'Just get out of my sight, will you?' he yelled at me.

But it was he who went first. I didn't realise until minutes afterwards.

I was left alone. I always had been alone.

We carried on avoiding one another, he and I.

Our instincts were primed, aware of every betraying pressure on the floorboards of the house, every creak.

Like this, I was thinking, we shall never meet, not a chance of it.

She didn't need to have you, but she did.

What was he telling me?

My sisters are dark, and I am fair. They have sharp noses, like their father, but mine is straight and even.

The differences have never seemed so clear and obvious to me.

*

'This is the way the ladies ride,
Jimp and small, jimp and small.'

My father hadn't known the rhyme as I did. But it wasn't he who had bounced me on his knees.

'This is the way the gentlemen ride,
Trotting all, trotting all.'

I had been in someone else's house, waiting for the all-fall-down, giggles already packed into my chest and just waiting to burst. While my mother watched, and Johnnie Melrose bounced me on his knees.

'This is the way the cadgers ride,
Creels and all, creels and all!'

I was walking along Heriot Row.

The fact is important (I clutch at details, at anything), only because the location was completely incidental, and yet it was the last place where life was truly 'normal' for me, meaning life as it had been.

A car is parked by the kerbside. I stop, bend forward, check something about my appearance in the wing mirror.

I find I'm really looking for the person I was, who I used to be.

The girl with the flaxen hair. Morven and Ailsa have dark hair, my father's was black before it showed grey. My mother's hair was light brown. Johnnie Melrose's used to be fair, and always bleached lighter in summer.

My own hair is fair. Like the Melrose girls', like Struan's.

My face is changing as I look at it. The eyes stare back with cold terror in them. The blood is visibly draining from my cheeks, my brow, the skin is bluey-white.

It has occurred to me in an instant. I'm not Ran Guthrie's daughter; my father is Johnnie Melrose.

Old friends. My father's best man. Godfather to the third daughter, who might have been an afterthought, last to be born and yet not the least.

And then, of course, the hammer swings for a second time, and this time I'm knocked flat. If I am that man's child, then I have given my virginity to my own half-brother.

I stood on the pavement until I realised I was starting to sway. I reached forward, clung on to some area-railings.

Reeling, I stumbled forward as my stomach heaved up its contents. There was a pool of vomit on the pavement, more of the stuff dribbled from my mouth, down my skirt and legs and on to my shoes.

My head was at boiling point.

I held on to the railings. Someone spoke to me; I waved him away. All that mattered now . . .

Johnnie Melrose, myself, my mother. How I had secretly loved the man who had helped to give me life. And the last taboo, passed beyond in the hotel bedroom.

My stomach flipped, my mouth filled with a sour taste. I spat the greenness out. I suddenly felt my legs were going to give way, and I slumped down on to the top step, outside the house of strangers.

In love with a forbidden man.

La-la-la.

Raped by kith and kin.

La-la-la-la-*la*.

My head was in my hands. A hand touched my shoulder. I couldn't look up.

I'll find you a taxi, the voice said, you look as if you've had a nasty shaking-up . . .

Oh, you've no idea, none at all. I wanted to laugh out loud, laugh all the houses down.

Instead I let him guide me to the taxi when it came, past my vomit puddle. The driver was sounding anxious; it was a new cab, new-ish, only six months old, just run in, and he didn't want any problems in the back. The man assured him, and closed the door, and I tapped on the window glass to thank him but couldn't bear to look him in the face.

I saw nothing at all of the journey.

Scene after scene from my life was passing in front of my mind's eye. Every point at which I had encountered Johnnie Melrose. At our home, at Hourn, at Moray Place, in the streets, at the theatre, at concerts, in Melvin's music shop, in Fuller's tea room.

Now already we were in Royal Circus, at the kerb in front of the house. I tugged at the handle, opened the door, stumbled out. I tipped the notes and coins from my purse into the driver's hand. Was that enough? I asked.

Too much, Miss, he was saying behind me.

I stared up at the house. What was I doing here? I had no reason now to be here. Here or anywhere. This wasn't my home; it never had been.

Your change, Miss –

I returned to the taxi, got into the back.

Wrong address, Miss?

No. Yes.

Somewhere else, Miss?

I had nowhere to go. Where *could* I go?

Melvin's music shop.

Melvin's music shop it is, Miss.

I was at the Debussy section among the racks of sheet music when everything caved in on me and I collapsed. One moment I was standing upright, the next I was lying on the floor. I was flat out on my back, looking at the ceiling, which was getting further and further away from me, receding and receding, while I was shrinking fast and had started to turn, turn, falling backwards all the long way back through time and space.

what can't be undone
there are storms on the moon
everything/nothing

No one can understand. They come into the room and leave again.

'She won't speak.'

Food is brought for me, on a tray, and left. Dr McCorquodale calls by, and returns with a colleague. Whispers at the top of the staircase; a door is closed downstairs and discussion begins in earnest.

I'm irredeemable.

what can't be undone
if but when maybe
the smile behind the smile

the girl with the flaxen hair

I don't sleep. I sit up watching the arcane libretto of stars in the sky. Galaxy beyond galaxy, ad infinitum. I can't imagine that, I can't picture it.

Perhaps *nothing* exists, then?

Don't I want to go out for some fresh air? It's been days, almost a week.

'What can't be undone,' I tell them.

*

There are storms on the moon. Up there.

'Now she talks at least.' 'But it's gibberish.' 'It's something.'

Time passes. Whole swathes of my life. Galaxies go tumbling into so much time.

'Why don't you play your music? Let me hear your music.'
(One), it was never *my* music. (Two), my hands are clenched, fingers rolled into fists. (Three), it's pointless anyway. Music is dead.

what can't be undone
let's drink to that –

– a glass of bubbly
there is everything, and then there is nothing,
nothing *is*
add on a question mark, curve your voice up

'Your mother lives on in you, Eilidh. You haven't lost her. She will always be there. A voice in your head. And when you look in the mirror. Believe me.'

> *'Lady, Lady Laders,*
> *Lady, Lady Laders –'*

A ladybird has landed on my wrist; now it's embarking on a long journey up my forearm.

> *'Take up your cloak,*
> *About your head,*
> *And fly away'*

I lift my elbow.

> *'Fly o'er forth,*
> *And fly o'er fell,*
> *Fly o'er pool,*
> *And running well'*

Another day, possibly.
Another ladybird, is it –

> *'Fly o'er living,*
> *Fly o'er dead'*

– on my dress, spreading its wings.

> *'Fly o'er corn,*
> *Fly o'er lee,*
> *Fly o'er river,*
> *Fly o'er sea'*

Suddenly the helicopter-motion spins it off, off and away across the garden.

> *'Fly you east,*
> *Or fly you west,*
> *Fly to him*
> *That loves me best.'*

I'm a 'she' suddenly. I hear myself being discussed as if I'm not in the room, as if I'm an absence.

She is to be treated at home.

There isn't going to be any outside help, thank you very much. Once professionals get their hands on you, and the disgrace is made public, then you're finished, finito, kaput.

*

[86]

'At home', only of course it isn't, but none of us is going to admit that. None of us speaks our mind, but mine – naturally, *un*naturally – is in no position to offer.

It's as if I have moonstorms inside my head. Dust and wind.

what can't be undone

A letter from Johnnie Melrose. So sorry to hear that you haven't been yourself, hurry up and get well soon, plenty to look forward to, we could have lunch one day if you like.
A letter from Johnnie Melrose, which I never saw again.

what can't be undone, can't ever be

My head is so frail; inside I'm carrying wine-glasses brimful of water and someone is playing them with a wet finger, until my skull is throbbing with the reverberations.

Played in water and glass,
the submerged cathedral, fathoms down and I'm looking up
the girl with the flaxen hair, hair winnowing about her head so prettily, like a drowned corpse

A castle by the forth. Ailsa's Ming has driven us here.
Scotland is a land of castles. Defenceworks, rebuffing our enemies, burdening ourselves with a siege mentality.
At the top of a dark, narrow turret staircase, there's a view quite unexpectedly out to open sea. I stand on the parapet for as long as I can, in the wind. I haven't tasted the salty Fife wind for months.
We have a picnic down on the rocky shore. They agree I look better for having got some colour into my cheeks. Ailsa

holds out her hand, she's wearing an engagement ring, they want me to be the first to see.

On the home stretch, being driven back to Edinburgh, I have a glimpse of myself, travelling in a different car and in the opposite direction.

Back to the beginning. Back to Go. Square One.
   La-la-la.

   what can't be
   There are storms on the moon

Nobody can understand.
   'She seemed all right when we were at the castle.'
   Something must have upset her.
   Or maybe it's Edinburgh, she needs a change of scene, but we'll wait a while, wait and see.

   wait and see
   see what we'll see
   across the sea

They've taken away my mother's clothes, the wardrobe is empty, and the dressing-table has been swept almost clear.
   The mirror stays empty, too.

   what can't be undone

Dr McCorquodale gives me tablets to help me sleep, and tablets for daytime, to take whenever I feel the wheels won't stop spinning in my head.

Wind drives the clouds fast. They bluster from the north, across a watery blue sea-sky. From the back windows of the house I can see the green of Fife, and now and then a curl of smoke – like the stave of a question mark – from the funnel of a ship as it passes up or down the Forth.

CHAPTER FIVE

Missing Person

M ost of all I think of getting away, following the cantering clouds south.

It's mentioned again, several times. 'A change of scene'. More good than harm. To take her mind off . . .

(Those suspension dots.)

Aunt Kit Guthrie blows in like the clouds, from Falkland, to look at me and to appraise the damage and the possible risk to herself.

She leaves. But she returns with a packed trunk.

Now everyone's talking about Paris. About Le Touquet Paris-Plage.

I do my own packing, discussing with Morven and Ailsa what I shall require. A suitcase instead, to contain my life in the smallest space. My life stripped, pared down to the essentials.

Edinburgh falls away. Spires, turrets, Ionic colonnades, the greystone terraces, the harbourside of Leith.

We've gone. Somehow we've put it behind us, or that's what I can believe. The sky is lighter already, the rhythm of the train's wheels on the tracks is hypnotically soothing.

Aunt Kit has opened a steaming flask by the time we reach the sandy links of Dunbar. ('Edinburgh Blend' tea, which she doubts the restaurant car will run to.) Intermittently she shows a gentleness which her brother, the one she calls 'your father', can no longer give me. I wonder if perhaps, after all, you can rebel against family and the blood libel.

*

But from London, from the Channel ferry, from the Pas de Calais, Edinburgh is never quite lost to us, and all that it signifies. It's like unfinished business. It's voices whispering at the back of my mind. It's a nudge and a wink. It's what can't yet be undone.

Briefly Paris looming eclipses other thoughts. In a wide sweep the railway line skirts the centre of the city. I watch for the landmarks: for Montmartre, for Notre Dame, for Gustave Eiffel's tower, the skylights of the Louvre, the Arc de Triomphe.

It's all confusingly familiar to me, as if I've been here before or as if I've dreamed it to life. And then my concentration slips just a little, and I'm trying to think where I'm remembering it from, from which photographs in which book or magazine, and the when and where of discovering Paris for myself the first time, more than six hundred miles away in Edinburgh.

The streets are like rivers, running with people, and I swim in them, with or against the tides. I dive in, defying the deeps.

I dive into the knowledge, into tides of blue. Every colour, every surface, is modulated by blue: white solidified to grey, blue turned denser (blue squared), green thickening to turquoise, red ripening to purple.

The details of the architecture are lost in the surrender to blue. Buildings become shadings; they interrupt but don't impede the victory of blue.

Continually there are reminders, traps.

It isn't possible to escape.

Cigarette smoke, for instance. Someone's perfume on the street, left behind as a kind of smear on the air. From a café doorway the aroma of coffee grounds, with that underscore of chicory.

It pains me, whatever it is. I ache, for I don't know what. I'm glad to have got away, and yet I'm uncertain just what it is I fear. I live in fear of *something*. I walk along the streets not thinking, afraid to put my foot down where I shouldn't, on an unlucky spot. Everything hangs and connects by a web, and I'm held.

* * *

Aunt Kit had taken me to the Louvre.

I was standing in front of a Watteau. *L'Embarquement pour l'Île de Cythère*. Lovers waiting to be ferried to their paradise island.

I heard a familiar name being spoken by a man's voice. A Scottish accent. Saying my own name.

'Eilidh Guthrie?'

I turned round. Stared. Into his brown eyes.

'Do you remember me?'

For a couple of seconds my expression must have been a blank, and the confidence started to drain away from his face.

I nodded.

'Colin Brogan,' he said.

'I remember.'

My voice sounded colourless, but he relaxed a little.

'What are you doing here?' I could only think to say.

'I suppose I could ask *you* the same.'

'I asked the question first,' I said.

'Well, coincidences happen. Don't they?'

Suddenly embarrassed, I looked back at the painting. I read out the title.

'But it's probably them returning,' he said.

' "Returning"?'

'From the Isle of Love.'

'It says "Embarkation".'

'That may be wrong.'

'How d'you know that?'

'I've read up about Watteau,' he said.

'Why?'

'Why have I read up about –'

'No, why is it not what it says? Why is it a return?'

'The light's fading, dying. And the figures are now in couples.'

I considered the human players again. Yes, you could reinterpret their conviviality as fawning and spooning: why else the infestation of cherubs wheeling about their heads. A statue of some goddess was gratefully garlanded in roses.

'Whereas they probably went over singly,' he said. 'Like pilgrims.'

I saw the point he was making. I nodded.

'Are you alone?' he asked.

Aunt Kit had gone off for tea to W. H. Smith's on the rue de Rivoli.

'For the moment,' I said.

He had dust on his well-worn shoes. Coincidences happen, he'd just said, but I guessed he must have been trailing us, through the Palais Royal gardens and along the paths in the Tuileries.

When I looked again at his face, it was through narrowed eyes.

'Are you here to protect me?' I asked, my voice ratching.

'From wrongly attributed titles, yes.'

I shook my head at him.

'It's not painful,' he said.

'What isn't?'

'To smile. It's allowed.'

'You don't know anything about me,' I said.

'Does that mean I've irritated you?'

[93]

'If it's what you want to think.'

'I hope I haven't.'

'Why?'

'I'd like you to have better feelings about me than that.'

'Ah, what you might *like*,' I told him, 'is another matter.' I managed a dry smile.

'Can I accompany you back?' he asked.

'Back where?'

'To where you need to go.'

'Aren't you clever enough to know that, too?

'I know you can't be in Paris by yourself.'

'I wouldn't stand much of a chance,' I said. 'With coincidences like *this* happening.'

He smiled, shrugged.

'My offer stands.'

'The rue de Rivoli,' I heard myself telling him, 'which isn't far.'

'You've seen enough in here?'

'I'm ready to go now.'

'Too much marble to walk. Marble saps energy –'

'Did you know you'd find me here?'

He didn't answer.

* * *

I only tell him that my mother has died, quite unexpectedly. And I've been a bit low, and I'm here in Paris to see somewhere new and to try to get myself better.

Aunt Kit has rung home, to check up on our companion.

He has been granted some grace, so no alarm bells were rung. She's easier in her mind now, because someone else will share the responsibility for keeping me amused. Her mood lightens, her spine straightens, and she leaves us smiling as she heads off for the shops.

'So, now what?' I ask him.
'Whatever you say.'
'Carte blanche, is it?'
'Don't ask me to translate!' he says.
'What are you here to see?'
'What d'you have in mind?'
'I asked *you* first,' I tell him.
He mimics Munch. *The Scream.*
'Well, we're on a bridge certainly,' I say.
It's the Pont Neuf, between the Quai des Orfèvres and the Quai des Grands Augustins.
'This isn't getting us anywhere, is it?'
'Yes, it is,' he answers me back. 'To the other side.'
'But *then* what?'
'Ah.' He's grinning at me. 'Back again?'
'Au contraire, M'sieur.'

* * *

He and I walk. Walk and walk.
We discover a city we half-know already. From the Bois de Boulogne to the Bastille, from the hinterland of Montparnasse to the Parc Monceau with its pyramids and obelisks.
Paris has become ours, entirely ours. It might have been created specifically for our diversion. A series of vistas and quiet surprises; street corners that have been waiting for decades for us to turn them. Cafés which are there solely because we want to sit and drink coffee: 'le patron' at the door, aproned waiters in attendance, coffee beans measured out and brewing in readiness, sun slanting in from the street

at that ancient and reposeful angle. All is suddenly, miraculously, a kind of perfection.

I can speak reasonable French, while he flounders. I know the difference between my perfect and past historic and imperfect tenses, I don't make mistakes when I give my order. I can scan the front page of a newspaper and use that as my cover, or lose myself in a menu.

I don't *need* to be available to him; it's my choice and a whim. I can consult a map, and I can also enquire about directions, I can make myself seem quite au fait with the city. I can dodge traffic, and jump on and off buses, and Paris might really be the closest thing to 'home' for me.

He remembers our conversations from Hourn, he quotes me, he has committed my words to memory.

I didn't know then that what I was saying would live on beyond that moment. I'm uneasy to hear my thoughts, delivered as they were off the cuff, now being spoken back at me. Why should he have wanted to remember?

I keep my distance, so to speak; at the same time I don't exclude him. It's a feat of coordination. Literally, out on the streets I walk a little in front of him, I lead, I give him the opportunity to follow, to keep up with me but always a couple of steps behind, where he can hear me but where I don't need to listen to him, pretending I haven't heard.

The blue light of Paris. We evanesce into it, into the gradations beyond, the lemons and pinks and violets.

He's bought a postcard of the Watteau.
   'I thought you disapproved of that,' I say.
   'Not at all.'
   'Why *that* picture?'

[96]

'Why d'you think?'

We sit under the trees in the courtyard of the Palais Royal.

The gardeners are laying the dust with watering cans upturned.

Shadowy figures pass along the silent colonnades.

I close my eyes, lift my face to the sun. For the first time in I don't know how long I'm not thinking of anything; my head is clear. I only realise a couple of minutes later when I'm returned to here and now – children's voices somewhere – and I feel the dull tugging of old, unresolved thoughts. I turn to see him sitting beside me, and I'm consoled to have him there.

I smile.

'I've given up smoking, Eilidh.'

'Why?'

'You told me to.'

'Is that what you want?'

'I want to *because* you told me to.'

'Oh.'

*　*　*

Once or twice our hands collided, his arm brushed mine, and I immediately backed away.

After that he took greater care.

He stayed by my side, but came no closer.

I didn't think I could wholly trust anyone, even Aunt Kit with those phone calls to Edinburgh. But I was in a different country now, and not quite the same person I'd been *back there*.

The sun was oftener and warmer, the air was lighter, and

you could believe in the possibility of new beginnings. It was easier to imagine that the same danger couldn't strike twice, not in the same way.

The terror I lived with now was of things GOING BACK, reverting. I wanted to keep in forward motion. On and on.

Once or twice I thought I saw Struan Melrose ahead of me on the street. Or, somewhere else, it was his father. His father and my mother, Lindsey Guthrie.

I couldn't get rid of them. They were able to materialise, even here. But when I heard *his* voice speaking instead, Colin's, I knew then that it was an illusion, the person I'd spotted wasn't who I had supposed, but just a chance resemblance, if even that.

I felt more confident precisely because he didn't know any of that past well enough for it to disturb him. It was accidental to him. Having him with me was like a talisman: maybe by association my past might become secondary, peripheral to me as well.

A tree. A table, a chair. Railings. Stone. A shadow on the ground.

He has to work fast.

'Before it disappears,' I tell him.

He works hard with crayons or watercolours to catch the essence of the object before it begins to change.

It's the opposite of how Ran Guthrie paints, that slow and systematic process of preparation – squaring off and plotting positions, pencilling and erasing before he's quite ready to dampen a brush, and only then to give himself a preliminary background slub.

I'm critical, but he accepts it. Having something to say

is a focus for me; it reins in thoughts that would go flying off somewhere else, it narrows me down to a necessary now. And that's just fine, in the light of all that's gone before.

* * *

I had a pebble in my shoe. We stopped and while I leaned against him, I removed my shoe and shook out the stone. All the time I was giving my attention to a poster in a travel agent's window. A view of steep white cliffs and a thin inlet of aquamarine sea.

SNCF – Voyez La France – Les Calanques

We had started to walk off when I turned back. I nodded to the poster. The searing white of the limestone cliffs in sunshine, the acid green of the Mediterranean. A moored white yacht, a tiny figure swimming past in miraculously clear water.

I loved the chance nature of this revelation. It seemed to me like a signal. Signifying I didn't quite know what. For days I had been coping with a sense that this world is saved from the morass of meaninglessness by what is in effect the opposite, strands of contingency and coincidence which weave together: like a dewy spider's web revealed on a hedge before the sun has dried it off, sometimes the pattern is observable but mostly not.

I continued to think of the poster during the day. I looked into the windows of every travel agency we passed, hoping to see the view again. It didn't reappear. But that must have been meant to be: leaving me to carry the image about with me in my head, making the special effort not to forget.

I realise that now. Now, when all the streets have been

walked down, all the pebbles of Paris which ever worked into my shoe have been shaken out.

I longed for sunshine, for the glare of full sunlight, for heat on my skin.

I was tiring of this tasteful blue light. But I was also afraid that this sojourn was bound to end, sooner rather than later.

I had grown up with the New Town legends, those exotics – the Edinburgh misfits and mavericks – who had escaped to the south, to fleshpot resorts where the dying revived and others continued their raffish ways.

There were degrees of southernness. Bournemouth, Torquay, Le Touquet, Dinard, Nice, Malaga, Tangier. Lack of money was no serious impediment, if the spirit was willing.

In the south, the north was turned on its head. Grey turned bright, wet turned dry, sobriety was softened, self-denial excused itself, old repressions were replaced by candour.

The south was buried inside every northerner, as a kind of birthright. But it had to be sought out, enticed to the surface.

If I run I can just keep clear, two steps ahead of whatever I don't want to think about, jumping over pavement cracks and potholes –

He grabs me, wraps his arms round my waist, holds me to him. People walking by look across: they expect to see lovers, here on the Boulevard St-Germain or in the Jardin du Luxembourg, Doisneau lovers from the photographs, and so they suppose that fate upon us.

But not quite yet.

* * *

I left a note for Aunt Kit. Not to worry about me. I wanted to see somewhere new. I wouldn't be travelling alone. I would try to keep in touch.

'South,' I said to him.
'South where?'
'It doesn't matter.'
'When?'
'Now. The next train.'
There was a train leaving on the hour for Avignon. We bought two tickets, one way not aller-retour. He carried my suitcase while I held on to his duffel-bag of brushes and paints.

In the compartment I took a seat facing forwards. He sat down opposite me, with his back to the engine. I was aware of him watching me, unable to take his eyes off me.

In the w.c. I splashed my face with water while I pictured the scene back in the rue de Babylone. Aunt Kit is opening the letter I've left for her, eyes wide as she speed-reads the lines to get the sense. Her mouth sets hard as she realises that this makes me a missing person.

Une disparue.

I smile back at myself in the mirror above the basin, the woman found again, I smile at the irony of this situation.

It was so simple, wasn't it? Bob along on the current, then make your jump; ride another current for a little while, until you're ready – any moment now – to jump again.

I had fallen asleep to the motion of the train. When I awoke, the window-blind had been lowered. I pulled back the corner.

Sunshine roared in at me across yellow sunflower fields, a Van Gogh summer, so brilliant – so violently bright – I had to close my eyes again and for several seconds I saw only long slow white flares dropping, one after another, sunspots falling.

Again.

I screwed up my eyes to see.

Sunlight everywhere, white light pouring into every corner. The hot air of Provence shimmered gassily. There were no jarring elements to upset the harmony of shapes and colours I was looking at. Everything fitted, belonged, and so suddenly – amazingly – did we.

* * *

A hotel in Nice. A double bed.

How is this with you? he asked.

Oh. Fine.

But we haven't talked . . .

He offered to sleep on the floor.

Don't be a chump.

The first time he touched me intimately, on my right breast, I froze.

A palm tree in the courtyard was slowly, slowly brushing its fronds against the wall.

Gradually I thawed.

It didn't happen that night, or the next, but on the third. I couldn't think of any more ways to hold out against him.

Are you sure, Eilidh?

Are *you*?

Never surer.

I told him, no, he wasn't the first.

You didn't say.

And I didn't ask *you*.

He sat sketching me. From the bed I watched him, from upside-down.

Do you want to tell me, Eilidh?

It's something I only want to forget.

He nodded.

What about you? I asked.

Oh . . . He shook his head.

He carried on sketching. He looked over and smiled gently.

I felt we had made ourselves an understanding.

CHAPTER SIX

Ports of Call

The Evidence

magnolia buds from a garden in Cimiez
a box of matches from the Hotel Negresco
a paperback copy of Jacques Prévert's poems
a cobbler's bill for fitting a heel back on to my shoe
two one-way train tickets to Menton
a coathanger from the Hotel Alhambra, Cap Martin
blue and orange pebbles from the beach at Beaulieu
envelopes and sheets of notepaper from the Hotel
    Leopold, Villefranche
a handful of hazelnuts presented to me by a stranger
wrapped sugar cubes from a café on the Promenade des
    Anglais
postcards of the Orthodox Cathedral in Nice
a timetable of ferry sailings to Corsica
a nail file
a business card: RIVIERA APARTMENTS TO RENT, ALL
    PRICES
a tariff of slot-in-the-meter electricity prices
entry tab to a public bains-douches
postcards of Antibes and Juan-les-Pins
an oleander flower, pressed between two sheets of tissue
    paper
a swizzle-stick from the Hotel Martinez in Cannes

*

That was the best time of all.

We lived according (just) to our means, and sometimes not at all.

He sketched passers-by on quaysides or walked from café to café looking for customers. Without telling him I sold the three-links Russian bracelet of my mother's, which had been *her* mother's. He had a couple of good wins at the Casino Ruhl in Nice, on games of rouge-et-noir.

Months passed.

Months passed like this.

He took little jobs – showing tourists how to sketch for themselves, decorating newly-fired plates in a kiln, even washing last night's dishes in a restaurant – so that I could sleep late in the mornings and he could paint me bathing and dressing and later walking about with him, or reading, or swimming.

[UNTITLED May 14th (1962)]
I'm leaning back in a chair. Sun shines into the room.
My cheeks and my bare forearms are the same
heightened colour as the peaches ripening in a white
compotier.

We flitted from hotel to hotel: from respectable to not, from pension to (now and then) grande luxe. We always paid our bill, but it might be that we were down to our very last francs and centimes. Occasionally we slept out, in the pine dunes or under an olive tree in a field, until we could afford another roof over our heads.

It wasn't quite real life. It was much superior to that. We

owned little more than the clothes we wore, and the two suitcases we hauled everywhere. There were only ourselves to keep fed and clean and healthy and happy.

I recognised the life in those grand hotels. The refrigerated atmosphere indoors, while outside the heat slammed down; the politesse of artificial friendships, the order of mealtimes and the straight corridors.

Here was my old life in institutional form.

No. He didn't think we should own things. Too bourgeois.

Objects ought only to serve our pleasure; we shouldn't be in thrall to them.

I saw the perfect sense of that.

If we required a car, he said, we should hire one, the latest model which wouldn't break down. If we felt like sailing, watching the land from the sea, we could charter a boat for half a day, or a whole day. No point in buying what demanded maintenance, and was destined to become obsolete anyway.

Typewriter. Radio. A portable record-player. Whatever, anything that could be paid for by the week.

We let a beach photographer have his way with us.

Two 'nouveaux venus' who can't stop themselves smiling. Leaning against a white picket fence, with a straw sun umbrella in the background, which belongs to the private beach next door.

We want a record of this moment, to be able to believe in it fully ourselves. Not the sun umbrella or the Tahiti bar. But just the *being here*: somewhere which is already being sneered at back in Edinburgh by those who think they know much better.

Side by side, arms touching, thinking how to be casual.

This is a magical place. Time is running backwards; they're growing younger by the day, soon they will be who they were a couple of years ago. The pair smile, from cheek to cheek, at the ridiculousness of metaphysics on a Côte d'Azur pleasure beach.

* * *

'D'you ever wonder what they're all getting up to?'
'Then I think of something else,' I said.
'What will they be doing?'
'Wondering about *us*, probably.'
'I expect I'm a great disappointment.'
'They would need to care first.'
'Don't they?'
'No one's come to look for us,' I said.
'A private detective?'
'In a novel maybe. Not in the New Town.'
'Why not?'
'Oh . . . A detective is cheating.'
'So, you wouldn't have *me* trailed?'
'No.'
'You trust me?'
'It's just that you don't waste good money on a mercenary, a sneak.'
He laughed.
'It's still there in you, isn't it?' he said.
'What is?'
'Edinburgh.'
'Less and less, I hope.'
'And that suits you, Eilidh?'
'It suits me very nicely indeed,' I told him.

*

No, I didn't want him to judge me by my family, or by those people we Guthries had conveniently called our friends.

Whenever he asked me, I told him less than I saw he wanted to know. To divert him, I asked him to tell me about *his* life, his history. He shook his head and said it didn't really matter to him now, it wasn't connected.

'If it doesn't matter, then you might as well tell me.'

'You'd get bored.'

'I won't know until you tell me, will I?'

I didn't recognise any of the dramatis personae, or the neighbourhoods of Edinburgh where they lived. The stairs up, and the communal wash-houses and back greens, the improvised ceilidh in a tenement close, the bed-recesses, things bought on the slate, his father's pal, the tic-tac man at the racecourse, and the trouble he caused, and the family having to go without, and a tally-man coming round every Friday to collect the instalments on their borrowing. How he'd spend hours in the public art galleries just to keep half-warm, and developing an interest in what hung on the walls of those austere foundations, and boning up afterwards in the City Library with its hot radiators and snoring readers, and hanging about the art colleges watching the students with their louche bohemian affectations.

I understood his life had a texture and density which I hadn't taken into account before.

He was also trying to make light of all the differences between us. I didn't want to undo the effort, when I really had nothing else to offer in its place. There wasn't anyone else willing to do what he was – to believe the best of me, maybe to redeem me in time.

*

What did happen to his father? I asked.

He'd gone out to get an evening newspaper. Down to the corner-shop, Ann's Pantry. Or perhaps it was for cigarettes. And he'd never returned.

Every so often they would hear about another possible sighting of him. In another part of Edinburgh, or in Dundee, or Glasgow, or Aberdeen. The sightings never led to anything.

They'd had to carry on without him, not knowing his whereabouts, or whether he was still alive.

Years later he wrote to them, out of the blue. No address, but a Manchester postmark. He was living with a woman called Joyce, they had a couple of kids, he wanted to say he was sorry but he'd known all along he could only be true to his nature.

'True to his nature.' For days, for weeks, the wife he had abandoned repeated the words, putting into her voice all the indignation and venom which she felt he deserved. She went about wild-eyed, the Medea of Fountainbridge. All that pity she'd wasted on the man. What she couldn't forgive him was the insanity of telling her; his feeble maudlin urge to speak for one last time, when she'd been quite reconciled to the notion that he must be dead.

She calmed down in time, but the letter was to alter her irrevocably. She changed her hairstyle, got new clothes, which must have cost a pretty penny. She spent a lot of time out with 'friends' she didn't talk about, came home with freshly applied toilet water which failed to quell the traces of drink on her breath and something else, the reek of male sweat that clung to her.

'It's a long sorry saga, Eilidh.'

Colin had his own life now. None of them knew he was in France. They had no interest in learning where he was, or what he was doing. That's how it is with some families, he said, and you have to get away if you're going to have a chance of surviving.

I hadn't told him about the dark side of the Guthries. He retained his illusions. But I signalled to him – with my hands, by letting him seal my mouth with his – that I comprehended his own situation very well.

* * *

We made no plans.

Whatever we did was decided by how much or how little money we had.

Other people had timetables for their lives. They ran by the clock, from one insurance premium or pension payment to the next.

We had different ideas, although it wasn't a proper philosophy: just an instinct for what *not* to become.

When we bought our food from shops or market barrows, it was always on the spur of the moment. (There shouldn't be any preparations beforehand, that was the one untransgressable rule.) Or we ate out, in restaurants, in cafés. Often we made do with stalls on the street and ate on the hoof: a crêpe fresh from the pan divided into two, or a bag of hot salted chestnuts between us.

Food answered our hunger pangs. For us it wasn't either a social ritual or a fetishistic exercise. We pleased our senses sometimes, on succulent fruit and melt-in-the-mouth pastries, which seemed to demand they should be consumed; but the eating was quickly over and done, and the evidence tidied away, as if we were secretly guilty in our presbyterian fashion, and there was pleasure, too, in that.

*

We listened to the radio. Music, mostly. He left the choice to me.

Chamber works. Lieder or chansons. Instrumental recitals. Opera.

If I recognised a piece, I told him what it was. I had amassed a lot of knowledge unconsciously at home, from the wireless or my mother's records, latterly from listening in record shops to something I'd heard Johnnie Melrose discussing.

[THE RADIATOR]
The radiator stands off in one corner of the room.

The heavy, insistent furniture is blocked in. But the wood has been faded by the sun, and the individual items lack definition.

The radiator becomes the focus of attention. It's the old-fashioned hot-water sort, coiled like a long alert serpent. A pair of woman's shoes rests on top to dry, riding the serpent's back. A shadow falls on the wall in such a way as to suggest a raised head: a brief trick of the Mediterranean light, animating the painter's imagination to produce this cowed phantasmagoric creature hi-ssss-ing.

Paints create a magic spell. It's as if no harm can come to us; our luck is holding. Into the woods and we'll defy the hazards that await us.

Walking into the Hotel Negresco in Nice, I was remembering Edinburgh's Caledonian Hotel. It took this Riviera landmark to remind me how luxury had seemed to a small child. The inert feel of carpet laid on top of marble, the curlicues of sound from a palm court trio, the delicious collision of perfume and cigar smoke in the air, the continual vigilance of well-trained staff.

I had been with my mother. She was leading me through the Cally by the hand. Voices rippled over discreet crockery effects. A melody from a stage-show. More atmosphere: the bell of a lift maybe, and cage doors opening, closing. A cake trolley being wheeled past. A fresh linen cloth being cracked open.

Why were we there? (That association in my head with perfume and cigar smoke, the tension in my mother's hand holding mine, the swish of new silk stockings, the staccato stutter of thin high heels.) And then, turning the corner – by a marble pillar perhaps – a man's familiar voice, a smile that won't be contained (faintly lopsided), hands held open. 'Mrs Guthrie! Why, fancy bumping into *you* here!'

* * *

I drop down into the sea water, so clear and deep that briefly I suffer a little panic attack of vertigo – there might be shipwrecks down there, or lost cities – until I start floating back up, raise my eyes to the rocks and the blazing blue sky.

In water I occupy again my three dimensions. I move free and unencumbered, with nothing to hold me.

I am.

I'm not anyone in particular, only a register of sensations. I don't have to prove or disprove anything. From second to second I change: I change shape, temperature, colour.

I AM AMorphous.

I was born out of my natural element, that's all. But every time I return there, I merge into it, I lose my mass and definiteness, I simply AM, this sensory organism, a presence of mind that reaches for miles and miles through time, to and fro, backwards and forwards, no longer one person but a mental *sponge*, and through its pores and runnels possibilities endlessly collude.

* * *

I asked Colin, didn't he want to return to Scotland?

'What on earth for?'

Here he had what he needed to paint, he explained, colour and light, brilliance and shadows; his head was continually filling with new ideas. His canvas life was an adventure, just as our own was.

'I'll go wherever *you* want to be,' he said. 'D'you want to go back?'

I shook my head.

'Then I think we should stay, Eilidh, don't you?'

Ports of call.

We put in, anchored ourselves for a few days, explored, wondered idly if we might want to stay here forever, then thought we might get tired of so much beauty, and so we weighed anchor, and (so to speak) set sail again, from this last to the next, where we would put in, anchor ourselves, explore, wonder idly if –

One hotel after another.

For a few days, sometimes for several weeks, depending. If he sells some paintings, if I can pawn another piece of my mother's jewellery. We may be down to our last £20, the fabled two £10 notes sewn into the lining of my suitcase, but something comes along: the hotelier's family wants piano lessons, or drawing lessons, or there's another little minding (the intermittent scholarship) from the Edinburgh Fathers, which somehow finds its way to us.

He grew a light beard. The hair on his head thickened out. His exposed skin darkened a little. Even when he was bleary and red-eyed from working so late, I saw that – in his heart of hearts – he was utterly content.

He lies beside me in bed. He lies on his flank, looking and looking at me.

I wait.

He reaches out his hand. It's a powerful hand, with strong fingers which look as if they could crush a paint-brush quite easily. But his fingers have the lightest touch as they trace the switchback of my body. I don't keep any part hidden from him.

The tip of his little finger approaches close, and that flickering contact with desire – the delicacy and finesse of his touch – has me aching for him. He must be able to hear the breath catching in my throat, the tiny spirtle-bursts inside my mouth.

I close my eyes, rather than have to see him looking at me, *his* eyes travelling over my surfaces, as if I'm a map unfolded in front of him.

Nothing concealed, and nothing denied him.

[UNTITLED]

X, who could be me, or possibly not. She is standing nude, wearing blue high heels, in front of the wardrobe mirror.

The room is a pastel wash of colours around her, the pieces of furniture have no clear relation to one another, they could be on contrasting planes.

What is reflected in the mirror presumably has a

clarity and order, a discipline, which the objects don't
have in the 'actual' room.

Owing to the mirror's angle, however, the nude's
reflection isn't shown. She stands staring in front of her,
looking to find herself. Her skin surface is daubed with
the quince yellow of the wall and the blue-green of a
chair. She is only very lightly edged around to
distinguish her from the swirling mélange of colours
which is the doubtful existence of the room.

Colin didn't bring the past any closer. When I was with him, it seemed to get further away.

He wasn't a nostalgist, which is usually the Scottish way. He enjoyed whatever was happening at the moment. If we talked about *then*, it was in passing. I felt we could both be *new*, here in this new place. We were those reflections in a shop's plate-glass window, or in the windows of a bus moving past us, but there wasn't much more to us than that. I was happy just to skim like that, to go scudding by.

I lie nude in the sun. My tan is all over.

On the shingle shore he makes love to me. His body is still pale compared to mine.

I am briefly the centre of the world; everything meets in me, at this one point. The sense of destiny builds and builds until the churning of shingle is the grinding of white stars, and my spirit is blazing across the universe, showering its pleasure as, oh, as asteroids and meteors, trailing sumptuous fire, and slowly slowly falling back to earth again to tell the fabulous tale.

* * *

Colin kept on painting me, over and over. Me against all the different backgrounds of our life then.

He never fully capitulated to the voluptuousness of the Côte. It's always there, but behind, in the background. The foreground is human, personal, domestic. Me.

It took a pair of northern eyes to see colour afresh like that, to become so enthralled by the southern light.

The washed-out ochres, honeys, roses. And the other sorts of colour which glow and burn, the fierce elementals, fixed with such startling clarity.

He had an aristocratic unconcern about the value of his paintings. He painted because it was all he wanted to do.

It was I who insisted. He had to get a dealer, he had to hold out for what he deserved, he ought to be ready to play one dealer off against another. I remembered how well my mother had adapted to the role of protectress, and now I had an opportunity to emulate her.

Never mind that they were representing Ran Guthrie, I decided to contact Rutherford McGavigan's. I wrote to Morven too, and asked her if she would follow my letter with one of her own, preferably using her husband's advocate's chambers notepaper.

Nothing is lasting.

Only my suntan.

We shed the pictures along the way. Some we sent off to Edinburgh, others were sold on the spot to pay our bills, and at least a couple were mislaid.

We received Sandy McGavigan's letters. I looked for evidence in them of Johnnie Melrose's single-minded energy. The prices seemed modest, and future hopes moderately stated. Maybe they were tolerating us only because Ran Guthrie was a client, because at Morven's prompting he had persuaded them not to abandon us.

'It's okay, Eilidh.'

'I wanted it to be better than okay. If he truly wants to, a dealer makes you covetable, he can convince his collectors to buy.'

I talked to him about trying London instead, but where would we start?

'It's okay, Eilidh. Really.'

* * *

Somehow we always put off the swimming lessons.

He couldn't do much more than he'd managed on those last couple of days at Hourn.

Maybe he wanted me to keep the mystique of swimming to myself, so that it would remain something *I* could do but he couldn't. He used the excuse of watching me and trying to capture the movements on his sketchpad.

He worked on a series of paintings of me swimming in the lido pool at Le Lavandou.

I was a body passing underwater, seen through all the surface reflections. A human form but, in that other element, elongated and sleek.

He would stand looking down into the water, dashing off his sketched impressions first, initialling in the colours he would use for painting later.

*

In these new pictures I'm dissolving into streaks of colour, patterns of light. It must be me, because whenever I looked up from the water he was watching. I search for clues in the finished pictures. Possibly it's my hair, maybe the turn of my cheek or chin. That yellow swimsuit.

* * *

Sometimes I wonder who he's talking to, just who he thinks I am.

We are also everyone else. Everyone else is us.

We slop over the edges of ourselves, we run into and mingle with others. The boundaries get worn away, and sometimes it's impossible to tell where 'I' end and 'you' begin.

Or how much of that 'I' and that 'you' is truth and how much is fancy.

* * *

He never properly learned French.

He used the shops where he didn't have to labour at conversation, where he could be understood well enough by pointing. Pointing with the lit menthol cigarette he's taken to smoking, to stave off the old tobacco craving.

I told him, that defeated the point of language.

'I communicate.'

'Not properly.'

'I speak to *you*,' he said.

'But if you don't use words –'

'What?'

I wasn't quite sure what I wanted to say.

'– there's one dimension missing, isn't there?'

'When I paint, that's enough.'

Meaning, he had the dimension he needed in which to express himself.

'You'd pick it up, the language.'

'You know enough for us both, Eilidh.'

'What if you have to do it on your own, though?'

'Like when?'

'I don't know.'

'Are you intending to go off somewhere?' he asked.

'No.'

'You're quite certain of that?'

'Why should I want to?' I asked him back.

'Just checking.'

'Anyway, who's said anything about going off?'

'I need to know you're happy,' he said.

'I'm fine, Colin. Rest assured.'

Bloody old Scotland, bloody presbyterian angst: don't enjoy yourself too much. Was that what we were talking about?

But then or later he didn't ever suggest to me, by what he said or how he behaved, that he wished we would pack up and return.

Anyway, go back to what?

Now that he's seen this light, he can't forget it. It has changed his view of the world. He has understood contrasts for the first time, absolutes of brightness and deep shadow; he has discovered tonality, perhaps the irrational also.

None of this can be *un*done. I'm connected with it in a disentanglable way: I'm the cause of it in one sense, it was I who brought him here.

*

'I love you so much, Eilidh.'

Even if he hadn't told me, it was simple to see, it was quite clear.

I didn't know if I loved him or not: whether I had the knowledge to love.

The fault lay not with him, I realised, but with me.

I could act the lover, play it out. I could make him believe I might very well be in love with him.

But to love means to give, to surrender. I was still bruised and sore, and very cautious. I was holding myself in, frightened to think what I might lose next time if I made the same mistake and trusted too much.

I parted with more of my mother's jewellery.

The settings were bulky and an earlier generation's taste, but the gold was heavy and high carat. The stones I already knew were good.

The luck of the objects, I felt, was starting to change. It was to break the bad spell that I was getting rid of them. They turned themselves into money, which guaranteed us our southern freedom here in the sun for a while longer.

I put silver varnish on my fingernails. On my toenails.

I sprayed on perfume. 'Vol de Nuit'.

I laid dried orange blossom among my clothes.

I was trying to leave little traces of myself behind, everywhere I went: the proof. Flakes of varnish, momentary overtones and undertones (jasmine, sandalwood), a capricious whiff of orange grove.

Smell is the most underrated of the senses. One day Colin was going to recognise a fragrance, in another situation completely – when he thought he was free of me – and he would be ambushed by something stronger than memory.

He will never lose me, I told myself. I am the man's Eurydice.

* * *

ivory black
burnt umber
Mars brown
Mars orange
Mars red
Indian red
or
Venetian red
cadmium red
yellow ochre
cadmium yellow
aurora yellow
zinc white
titanium white
viridian
terre verte
cobalt blue
French ultramarine
Winsor blue
manganese blue
blue black
cobalt violet
Winsor violet
permanent violet

Colin worked and worked at the sea. How to catch its constant static motion, and the way the sun breaks up, smithereening across its surface, laying its exquisite melancholy on the water. (Sometimes the foam thins out, running like streaks of fat in meat, or like time-cracks in leather.)

Against the sea, a cello back, which must be mine.

Has my hair discoloured so much?

In the sea, caught beneath the surface, a harmonious disturbance of the water, a swimmer in her element, just recognisably fair-haired.

CHAPTER SEVEN

La Croix du Sud

I n Hyères the air smelt of the carnations growing in the fields roundabout.

The palms on the streets lent the town élan.

He asked me, between a hardware shop and the post office, shouldn't we get married?

It was an absurd question. I should have laughed out loud. I should have told him, you've got heatstroke, I've never heard of anything so ridiculous.

Instead I heard myself saying, 'Yes, Yes all right'.

A crazy question deserved a crazy answer.

We might have been going about just another day's errands in the town, except that we were due to call in at the bureau de l'état civil, the registry office.

We found our witnesses in the street. I used my mother's wedding ring for my own.

Such casual matter-of-factness. In and then out. No false sentiment. Over and done with.

Afterwards we bought our witnesses green absinthes in a bar, and we got a little unsteady ourselves, drinking on our empty stomachs.

The two of us, husband and wife.

We took ourselves off in the evening for a meal. Neither of us said it was to celebrate; we didn't discuss what difference being married now made to anything. The evening as ever was warm, the air thrummed, the colours in the little garden of the restaurant became fluorescent. We seemed just how we had been on all the other evenings.

A moth fell into the glass lantern on the table and was frazzled; somewhere in the middle distance a dog barked.

How clever we were: treating marriage with the lightness and insouciance that was fitting, calling its bluff. Of course we didn't really believe in the institution, we were simply going through the motions, just to prove that what could be so unthinkingly done oughtn't to be treated with any more seriousness.

Or something like that.

*　*　*

We saw the names of the islands that lay due south. Porquerolles, Port-Cros, Levant.

Les Îles d'Or. The Golden Isles.

We told ourselves, if the weather held, we would go there.

Perhaps if we had taken the right road, the one we'd meant to take, to the Golden Isles . . .

There, we might have discovered our contentment, and I would have been settled in my mind, and he would have painted harmless pictures of me easy in my easy mind, just as content as *he* was, and in that case none of what was to follow would have happened . . . It would have been a story-book ending: or, rather, a story-book beginning to an alternative existence, which we might still be living together, so blissfully unaware.

[LA LECTRICE]
The outline of a woman fits the contours of her armchair. Her shoulders rest against the chair's shoulders, each elbow nestles into the crook between the arm and the back of the chair. Her thighs sink into the cushion, the

flesh-tone of her legs corresponds to the blond wood of the chair's turned legs.

A posture perhaps of solid middle-class comfort. But what is she reading, between those blue covers? What new thoughts are infiltrating her head?

Leaving Hyères, we took the wrong turning for the islands. Right instead of left.

We'd gone eleven or twelve kilometres before we realised. Inland, instead of down to the coast.

We could have turned back. But by now the sky looked lowering out at sea. Ahead of us the sky was, still, white clouds on blue. Ahead of us the roadsigns promised Marseille, the Route Corniche, Les Calanques, Cassis.

* * *

We drove downhill into Cassis.

The road led us gently on our descent, for two or three miles. The soft air had a charge in it, as if there was thunder in the offing. The old trees were shaped by winter winds.

I wound down the window. I smelt the tang of pine, confused with the sweetness of oleander.

Somehow I felt that I was coming home. I was looking at a new and strange place but with quite familiar eyes.

I sensed that *he* was ready to stop for a while, too.

Fishing boats were setting out for a night's trawling. The locals stood on the harbourside watching, smoking, turning round to look at us, nodding to us in a mystified but friendly way.

It was the start of something else: a drawing-in on ourselves.

He said, didn't I think the same thing, *it was time*?

*

[125]

The agent took us to see three houses that were to let.

The third was called 'La Croix du Sud'.

It stood at the top of a steep lane. It had a chalet roof: as if it was intended to be somewhere else, closer to the cloud line and with a view of snow. A sloping garden of palms and cacti. A high grey perimeter wall, with the plaster peeling off it, and a green wooden gate in the wall with a tarnished brass bell and clapper.

'La Croix du Sud'. I liked the name, it seemed fortuitous. Southerness – misfits and mavericks – the stuff of those Edinburgh legends.

The south was inside, but we had to search it out; the spirit must be willing.

'It was the only house with a piano,' Colin said on the walk back down the lane.

'Is that important?'

'It must have a piano.'

'Why?'

'The first time I saw you, at Hourn, you were playing the piano. I have to give you that.'

An upright Velland & Metzger. It needed tuning, but it had once been a fine instrument.

He said, he didn't want to deprive me of anything I'd had before, which would be subtracting instead of adding to my opportunities. I laughed and asked him, did he really think I was going to be at a loose end?

'Something for your mind,' he said, 'to keep it sharp.'

* * *

It took some adjusting, exchanging novelty for a routine. We weren't going to be distracted any more by other people, those bit-players who provided disposable atmo-sphere wherever we'd landed up.

I sometimes missed our portable domesticity.

But it would have been tempting fate, to think it must continue like that. We would have got to the point of feeling that we were repeating ourselves; what had begun by being spontaneous would have seemed more and more like a kind of obligation.

We'd had to make up our minds to suddenly give it up, or we might have grown too superstitious about our luck running out to know when to stop.

Slowly a rhythm of life did develop. We fell into it, without any foreplanning.

He painted, and I kept the house and tamed a garden.

Now he could lay things out, work with his materials spread around him. This way he could tackle several paintings at the same time, and consider them for longer.

His subject-matter would be to hand. He could record the same rooms and the same objects in different lights, differ-ent weather, however the mood took him.

I wanted him to work, and to feel that he could. He gave me all the credit for creating an atmosphere where he was able to concentrate, free from interruptions.

In the morning he got up early, opened the shutters, while I dozed on. He went downstairs, to get the room where he painted set up. He returned with my breakfast. I ate sleepily while he sat watching me, talking to me, smiling.

When he'd gone I lay on for a while, studying the reflections on the ceiling. Water in the jug, leaves of vegeta-tion. The ceiling would gradually whiten. I felt that my life had been washed clean; I had been given a chance to start it afresh.

[THE TIN TABLE]
The unexceptional table, made from some thin metal,
came with the house. A round top, a three-legged base
with three spindly arching supports. Old blue paint
revealed the base metal beneath; the top was dented and
off the straight.

This was where we most often ate, out in the garden.
I did my odd jobs there, and wrote on it with a piece of
folded card wedged under the base.

On the table-top, a yellow kitchen bowl, an open
book with pages fluttering, two halved lemons, a knife.

We speculated who might have lived here in the house before us.

We had no clues. The only traces left behind were scuff marks on woodwork and faded stains on carpets and upholstery which hadn't scrubbed out.

There was an inventory, a long list of every item supplied with the house. I took it about with me, from room to room, checking every object against its description, one by one by one.

The house itself is something solid to have around us, to root us maybe. Furniture to learn how to steer ourselves around in the dark.

But there's still the haunting presence of those previous occupants, a cryptic edge to everything, where information runs out. The solidity is dense and reliable – but only up to a point.

Which is fine. It saves us from turning into the sort of people, the arrant bourgeois, we don't want to be.

* * *

We drink the dry white local wine. I feel we're communing in some essential way with the place; it's physically entering into us.

Les Calanques.

Creeks, fjords, deep inlets forged between the whitestone cliffs.

Fissures deep-vein the gradients, which are sometimes nearly sheer drops.

The sea runs into caves. The water is blue over green over indigo.

The deeper the sea, the more placid it looks.

When the sun goes in behind clouds, the cliffs turn grey and, where the spare covering of pine trees casts deeper shade, purple.

Some nights, from way down the coast, I hear the fog-horn where the Cap Croisette lighthouse keeps watch in the dark, on its stern spit of rock.

Trees struggle gamely to survive in this blatant, unsparing heat. The heat, I'm aware, is making us economical with our movements.

Even so, we're determined to reach those private places on the cliffsides. We scramble over slithering scree to get there.

Two, three leaden-skied days occur in a row. The sea frays against the cliffs; the breakers implode into spume, a fine obliterating mist of spray.

Along the coast pleasure boats are smashed, a brief debris that disappears from view.

Branches snap off the old pines, spin into the air like blades.

Close to us, in the confined coves, the fury of the sea now boils up orange.

* * *

Colin asked me to play the piano for him. He said he liked to hear the music spreading through the rooms.

I tried my Edinburgh repertoire, but my mind locked, jammed. My hands clenched, my fingers wouldn't move.

I didn't want to disappoint him, though.

I wrote off for some music and learned pieces that had no associations for me.

Liszt. Albeniz. Scriabin.

It was music which I could move along the surface of; the way I played it, it had no depths. I gave an appearance of finesse and technique, putting on a show.

He listened, and said only complimentary things, he was the easiest audience I could have had.

I tried not to think about all the practice it had taken to get here, to be able to play with so little feeling. The untold hours of practice, the drudgery, just so I could end up performing a clever and sincere-sounding lie.

[LA SALLE À MANGER]
I'm sitting at the dining-table, writing.

The shutters are drawn against the brilliant sunshine.

The slats stripe the room with their shadows, they ripple diagonally over the wall and the floor and the back of the chair; on the chair seat and the table cloth they change direction, towards the perpendicular. I'm striped by the shadows too, so that I become part of the chiaroscuro pattern.

Look closely to find me, and there I am: a ground for the shadows, which then deduct alternating stripes of me

– I'm only defined by my clothes (blouse and madras check slacks). I'm shredded into a magma of colours.

The deeper shadows of my shoulders and head drop forward on the wall, I'm hunched and tense, covert; nose and chin softened to feline dimensions, I'm a cat hiding out in the long grass.

Or –

The legs of the dining-chair as they descend curve inwards, then taper out again.

They're the legs of a slender horse, a striped horse; I'm riding a zebra bareback.

* * *

I continued to swim.

As often as I could. At least once a day, but more if it was possible.

The limestone cliffs were searing white against the green sea and blue sky. If I closed my eyes, all I could see were avalanches of white crumbling mountain.

The water is deeper than it appears. The view from above can't hold all its depth. There are channels beneath, and further caves under those. Where everything is deceptively clear and transparent, the light is playing its tricks. The visible merely masks the invisible.

He would only get confident in the sea, I told Colin, if he accepted that he was bound to sink under several times first. But I would be there to bring him back up.

He still wasn't sure, he said.

'Well, it's only to help you. Tell me when. Tell me, and I'll help you.'

He learned enough just from watching me to keep himself afloat, and then to attempt a haphazard breast-stroke, to paddle on the spot with feet and hands as flippers. He would tell me where he wanted me to swim to, which allowed me to go off and leave him. A few times his attention wandered and he got out of his depth; I would look round, hearing him pound the water, sometimes I headed back, but – with some shouted instructions from me – he always managed to make his own way to a shallower stretch.

In the coves the shingle might suddenly drop beneath you, and even keen eyes and clear water couldn't keep you right about where the trenches lay. Just remember, I said, be careful, but I didn't want to nag him about it, from my unassailable wisdom, at the risk of hurting a man's pride.

* * *

[PLENTY Originally, THE REPRIEVE (title painted over)]
A table spread with an emerald linen cloth and loaded with fare.
   A woman sits at the topmost left-hand edge of the table, half-turned away as if her presence is being required somewhere else.
   The food is spread out like an offering, a thanksgiving.

Somehow making love seemed most natural in the garden, beneath the sky, on the warmth of stone or grass. I imagined my fingers intertwining with the branches of the Chinese nutmeg tree, citrus perfumes wafted over me in waves, I was rooted to the soil but my head rested among the stars.
   I told him. 'Very purple, isn't it? The sky.'

'Sort of violet, I'd say.'

We agreed on violet.

Purply prose, but a violet sky.

All the garden's past summers seemed to be contained in its old mellow stone, in the baked earth, in the sturdy gnarled growth, in the unstoppable perfumes. Ancient and triumphant, benevolent, and somehow dedicated to the feminine.

* * *

For a spell I did try teaching piano.

I advertised my services in the town, and a handful of students came up to the house: children brought by their parents, a few housewives, a businessman and an older widower.

The women wanted a social skill, the children weren't there by choice, the men were indulging a fantasy.

I got to dread hearing the bell on the wall and having to make my way down the garden to open the green gate and offer an encouraging smile.

But really I was dreading having to see myself where they were, facing the middle of the keyboard and obeying commands. Memories of Miss Marjoribanks's sitting-room and the Academy practice-rooms came hoving back into view, just when I thought I had exorcised them.

My successes were the pupils I persuaded to give up: some who had been sent without having any say, and others who were using their lessons to get back at parents or siblings. I saw that one or two, who did have some talent, needed a more experienced teacher to guide them, but I also found their ambition sterile: as if this activity was meant to replace some of the ordinary human transactions of life.

I wasn't popular with the parents for telling them what I

did, and demand for me fell away. But I realised that the children were grateful to me, or they would learn to be. I had got there before them; I could tell them things, from my other side of the mirror, about how youth and its optimism can be corrupted.

Colin saw how the business was making me despondent, and it was he who suggested I should stop altogether. I blamed the weather, mistral blasts, the twin effects of heat and sea on the piano's hammers and wires, our distance from a music shop, some pupils' unpunctuality, didn't the sounds of stumbling scales distract him from his work?

He suggested again that I should stop, more seriously on this occasion, and I didn't have to be asked a third time.

[UNTITLED (Incomplete)]
I'm bending down for something, beneath the level of the table-top.

To begin with, I'm lost against the carpet. Then I surface, like a tiger, the rust and wavy black lines I'm wearing now gilded and matching the sunlit sanded floor.

Again he talks about the Îles d'Or. We should go. That wonderful name, how could we not think of going?

But again I find reasons – trivial domestic reasons, or the weather forecast, or a delivery date he's promised Rutherford's – why, really and truly, it's impossible for us to go now or for the next wee while.

I'm afraid to go, in case the name is too perfect to be true.

I'm afraid of not knowing any other place to dream of going to.

I'm afraid that we're putting too much hope into this, and

that the experience might be too frail. I'm afraid of giving in to fears too easily.

* * *

Colonel Wootton further out on the headland has kept up the custom of afternoon teas at 'Villa Karnak'. Scones, strawberry jam, stiffly whipped double cream, 'Queen Mary' tea.

God knows where the produce came from; he gave the impression it was the most natural thing in the world that we should be sitting there, being so remarkably British under the rabid sun, with our damp clothes sticking to us.

He didn't care much for painting, or for the arts in general. He enjoyed the sound of British voices, though; he found Colin difficult to follow sometimes, but he accommodated us because I spoke a recognisable Queen's English and because we both provided him with an audience.

* * *

On our walls Colin has hung a dozen pictures, none of them completed. He needs a ladder to reach a couple.

He goes from one to another to another.

This is how Van Gogh meant *his* canvases to be seen: en masse, each in relation to every other.

The field has become flatter. Perspective is more enigmatic, ambiguous. Walls and tables and chairs and rugs and curtains and fireplaces meld into one another.

Differences and distinctions are ironed out.

'I used to look at the photographs in the library books,' Colin said, stretching out on the parched grass. 'The Scottish Colourist lot, when they came over to France. I never for one moment imagined . . .'

From beneath he set my hammock gently in notion.

'So,' I said, 'this can't be something you pictured?'

'No, I suppose not. The house, the garden.'

'Oh, they're real enough,' I told him.

'You're sure of that, are you?'

'Well, I thought I was . . .'

He laughed. Pushed again on the hammock.

'We can't both be mistaken,' he said, 'can we?'

I didn't answer. In the noonday heat, who could be quite certain about anything?

'The Colourists wore suits and ties and lacing shoes, I remember.'

'You would like a little more formality,' I asked, 'is that it?'

'I'm happy with things exactly the way they are.'

'Ah.

'Very happy, Eilidh.'

'Ah.'

'Aren't you?'

I leaned forward in the hammock, perhaps to swat at an insect. It meant I was unable to reply; it meant I didn't have to toil in the heat to discriminate, to particularise between a small truth and a little lie.

* * *

In Cassis town I passed a poster for a circus, pasted to a wall. In the illustration a girl was negotiating a high wire.

I walked past the girl every day. She had a quiet smile on her face. I thought the smile had a different meaning on different days. Intense concentration, assurance, to conceal her vast terror, or proof of her recklessness.

I searched for a nobler purpose for myself.

Fauré's piano music. Poulenc. Proust.

Maybe I lacked the mental energy, on those hot afternoons when the air poached you in a bain-marie. Or it might have been that I didn't want to start drawing on my reserves of useful projects: there should always be time, unlimited time, to finally get round to them. I wasn't ready to *shrink* time, not just yet.

New pictures, and the paint is barely dry.

She is nude, the woman, naked to the world. She has no privacy. She squats to dry herself, in all her animal unconcern. She has no shame.

The nakedness is somehow unerotic. She isn't advertising her attractions, she's ignoring the spectator as she continues with her ablutions.

In the later pictures I am unerotic because Colin paints me indefinitely. I'm losing my geography of curves and concealments. My breasts, buttocks, thighs are smoothed out.

I interrupt light like a prism, sunshine shatters and its colours run over me.

That is my function: to perplex, not to entice. Discovering it is a disappointment and a relief. I'm relieved that Edinburgh won't be embarrassed to know who this woman is, but I'm disappointed that he practises his skills in depicting light by using my naked body as a neutral conduit.

Colin asks what's puzzling me. I smile as I tell him, in an approximate way, what has occurred to me.

He looks at the canvases again and again, but it isn't clear to him what I mean. I say to him, oh well it doesn't matter, but with a smile that's now a little less than it was, in a doubting tone of voice.

He continues to look between me and the pictures.

We return for tea with the colonel.

We sit under a banyan tree on his terrace, and he reminisces about an England that no longer exists. He invites us to swim in his pool, but the tiles are cracked and there's a scum on the water, and it's easier just to let him talk, wait for him to open a bottle of his favourite burgundy.

It makes Colin and me feel we're being convivial and not entirely selfish with our time. We see one another in a social situation, and I hear myself – when I can squeeze a word in edgeways – expressing an opinion about a subject we've never discussed before. I say 'we', 'us', 'our', and that's confirmation of a life I share with my husband.

We stop at the point where to say something would be to give away too much of ourselves to a total stranger.

We clam up on our secrets. And naturally I have to wonder what the colonel's are, always talking about his England but – exiled like us – never returning there.

I received Christmas cards from Edinburgh. One from Morven and Alasdair, one from Ailsa and Ming, and the third from Sandy McGavigan. Nothing from Royal Circus.

I sent a card each to Morven and Ailsa. I didn't feel I had anything to say to either of them, no message, so I signed my name – not Colin's, why should he get embroiled? – and I left it at that.

I was acknowledging them as a formality. I had moved too far away from them. My life was private. I had too much to want to keep to myself. I found it more and more difficult to remember even what they looked like, nor could I recall the sound of their voices. I felt I must be escaping from them at long last.

Moths at night come battering at the windows. They're bigger moths than any I've ever seen, the size of saucers.

In the distance, dogs howl. Dogs on chains; necks fretting against metal collars.

But if you can ignore the noise and see *beyond*, to the pure crystalline beauty of what's above us – stars are scattered infinitessimally across a vaulting Mozart sky.

* * *

[INTERIOR AT 'LA CROIX DU SUD']
A rumpled bed. The silk slip thrown over the back of a chair, and a towel dropped on the seat. A tub of talcum on the table, with the lid beside it. A book lies open on the window sill, pages riffling in the suggestion of a breeze.

There is movement of sorts in the picture: a draught from the garden, and – implied – the passage of a person only a few seconds before from one room to another.

*Attention remains fixed on **this** room just left, as if a return is anticipated.*

Imagination sees a few moments ahead, to the sound of feet in espadrilles, and in this process of anticipation the invisible woman lives more realistically than if she was shown rising from the bed or discarding her slip.

Colin still made love to me in the garden, in the places where we used to, but now I didn't experience it as a liberation.

As discomfort, chiefly.

The vegetation had become more overgrown in the interim. I felt I was snared by branches and trailing tendrils.

I imagined that the papery rustling I could hear was the scuttling of lizards only a few feet away from my face. I had the sensation of insects running over my ankles, along my legs and arms. I pictured the bristling cacti at the far end of the garden, by the wall.

In the deep-green shadows neither of us properly saw the other.

I wondered if anyone could hear us from the lane, how many scratches I would be left with, and was supper going to spoil, would there be any supper at all since my preparations had been interrupted?

There were always things to be done. A puritan lived on in me, afraid not to be able to account for all her time, needing to be busy. The devil makes work for idle hands. I needed to know that something else was waiting to be attended to, and to hone my mind right down to it.

[LA PLONGEUSE]

An explosion of water. White spikes, like a hot-house pineapple, or a fool's cap.

The figure could be male or female, or only half-human. The colour of skin or hide emerges only gradually from the silver-blue water. A triangle of head, a portion of a back, the distorted angles of arms or paddles.

A shadow arc goes trailing beneath.

They say that death is a release; it's like travelling towards a radiant beacon.

Maybe swimming was an intimation of what awaits us. The water's resistance was overcome, there was nothing to hold me; no bright consuming flare, but it was here and really only here that my thoughts could attain the stasis of calm, a kind of serenity.

* * *

The longer I look, the more evidence I see in the rooms of previous occupants.

More marks on the walls, stains on the carpets and fabrics, scratches and chips on the furniture.

Two hollows in the mattress are the impressions of past hopes and disappointments, afternoon pleasures and midnight recriminations.

It's still a shock for me to glimpse that woman in the mirror. She seems like an intruder in the house.

The person who I think I am doesn't grow any older. I'm the age I was walking from the car to Miss Marjoribanks's, or when I met Johnnie Melrose on windy George Street, or running into the briny Atlantic at Hourn, or chasing the blue light in Paris. Everything is happening simultaneously, over and over, time without end.

Colin watches me drinking my coffee. I become awkward, knowing that each of my movements is being studied. I'm thinking about my actions, and so they aren't natural any more. My arms are heavy, my hands ungainly. *Her* arms, *her* hands. *She* looks ahead, fixing on the view without seeing it. (A great cubed head, with wide eyes, each on a different plane, and a nose like an escalator.)

Into the sky. The blue sky. Endlessly blue, azure, it rules these days. A generosity, a profligacy, of light.

It had seemed so easy. Catch a train. Jump up on to the carriage. Follow your star. As if there's nowhere you can't escape to, as if there can be 'impulse' without claims and penalties attached.

And you end up written into a story you don't realise is actually about you.

Beneath water Colin can't follow me. I'm alone, in my element. I streak away, impossibly streamlined, I swim for many miles.

Some alluding hieroglyphs on a canvas, a trail of motion in the water, a brief disturbance colliding with sunlight, that's all.

When the mistral comes, I lie low in the house.

I'm full of dissatisfaction for a few days.

The wind smells stale, it would be liverish yellow if it had a colour, it runs round and round on itself like a mangy dog chasing its own tail. I'm heavy, I ache, I don't feel like eating, I'm hot and cold at the same time, Colin lets me have the bedroom to myself, and I can see what he's thinking, does this mean that two are going to become three?

I have to wait for the weather to change.

The wind finally does an about-turn, and blows back the way it's come.

I allow Colin back into the bedroom. He offers no complaints about his treatment. He's gentle with me. I don't want him to be, his anger might kickstart me, and then I would respond with stronger emotions, and maybe that way – who knows – I would discover what passion is.

* * *

. . . Ming's thrilled, and says he doesn't mind if it's a boy or a girl. (Given that there were 3 of us, I don't know what the chances of a BOY are, do you?) Anyway, I wanted to tell you a.s.a.p.

Morven is delighted, she says she'll organise a christening for us, but I just have a sneaking suspicion she feels a wee bit upstaged.

Apart from this – !! – all goes v. well this end. Ming is always getting invited on to medical panels, so I don't always see as much of him as I should like. Even his fellow 'rugger-buggers' (their term, not mine) are complaining he can't train as much. But that's what comes of marrying a brilliant man, I suppose. (Totally unprejudiced comment, that!)

How're things in the sun? I don't really get to do the galleries and showrooms these days, but Morven pops in now and then, and she says she sees Colin Brogans quite regularly, so we know you're still living the locust-life down there.

We had a wonderful sunset yesterday evening, out over Ardnamurchan. I was reading somewhere, Scottish sunsets are out of this world. So, some things can't be improved on by distance, you see – they were here on your doorstep all the time!

[LA PLONGEUSE 6]
The swimmer is stretched beneath the surface of the water, in crazy-angled sunshine – elongated, distended, and fluidly imprecise – pallid, like some creature which avoids the light, with the blue and yellow stripes of her/ his costume like a shell – arms tapering inwards, pincer-like, flipper feet – not herself/himself, not at all, headless, and not even recognisably human.

Colin was pleased with the result. I didn't know how to criticise what he was showing me. I could see it was a clever exercise. He had caught very well the momentary shimmer of contending reflections. Again, it was the treatment of his subject which bothered me. I wondered why he should have wanted to paint me like this. Or wasn't I the point at all now, and it was solely the *effect* which mattered?

I lie soaking in the bath-tub. I lie quite still, holding my breath. The house is as silent as a tomb.

Reflections through the water glisten on the walls and melt their hard surfaces.

Death, I sense, is bright, sunny, casual in coming: a state of eternal unchangingness, with emotions put on hold. Fear may be unnecessary.

My own wisdom fills me; I float free, levitate a little, buoyed on my immaculate little cloud of knowing.

* * *

'Mrs Brogan, can't I tempt you? Another scone?'

'No, thank you.'

Some of the Cassis group have been invited over to 'Villa Karnak'.

A meddlesome American couple retired from the news-paper world. Two Canadian self-styled 'spinsters', who played for many years in the same orchestra. An Irishman, who has possibly lost a family fortune in the Riviera casinos. A south London garage-owner's widow; she seems a little déclassée for the colonel, but she wears sleeveless low-cut dresses and has a habit of running the tip of her tongue over her top teeth and laughs freely at our host's so-so puns.

Colin and I are a whole generation younger than the youngest of them. I don't know what we might have in common.

'They're not a sin.'

[144]

'Excuse me –?'

'The scones.'

'No, thank you. Really.'

'Have to keep up your strength, Mrs Brogan.'

Do I? For what?

For just more of the same. For this smiley chatter. For keeping house, and the daily walks down into Cassis, and my bathtime levitations, and willing the phone *not* to ring, and watching my nails grow, and opening windows to let out the breathless smell of paint and white spirit, and doing it all over again if that means I can hold at bay the shadows inside shadows.

The frivolous widow has her hand on my arm.

'Someone's just walked over your grave, dear?'

'What?'

She laughs at my surprise.

'Such a long face. And here we all are, living in paradise!'

I aim a smile at her.

'Oh, one smile doesn't fool me, you know. But six out of ten for effort.'

Damn your eyes. But I smile all the more sweetly to appease her. She isn't as fluffy-headed as my first impression of her was. How could she be, with her several admirers of either sex dancing attendance.

'Paradise is other people,' the eavesdropper Myra Betts says, and her trombonist friend Denise nods agreement.

'I thought that was hell,' says Elizabeth Grumbach in her Brooklyn drawl. 'Sartre.' She likes to remind us with her literary allusions that she is an intellectual, or considers herself as such.

'God's got us at it even here,' Lorcan Fadder with the stage-name groans in the too-true brogue he has grown into. 'Paradise this, purgatory that. Never gives your conscience a moment's rest, the old rascal.'

Can these people really be our friends? Colin doesn't care for them any more than I do. But we force ourselves to put in an appearance, in case we come to live too much apart from others. It just happens to be *this* motley collection of people we find ourselves shackled to.

'Trouble with paradise is keeping it a secret,' Denise Bertaux with her trombonist lips says, and her companion Myra nods.

'Trouble *in* Paradise,' says Maurice Grumbach. 'That was a film, wasn't it?'

'Opiate of the masses, cinema,' says the colonel, who has a Nietzchean view of the world without having read a word of the great man.

To *them* this politesse is sophisticated and urbane. We two are their tame bohemians. To oblige, I wear a chunky wooden bangle on either wrist, and Colin has somehow got paint streaks smeared on his cream linen trousers.

Toot-toot-toot. Fol-de-rol.

Click my fingers, and we're back at our villa with green shutters, and you're a queasy fancy I must have dreamed up on a cheesy lunch, falling asleep afterwards in the siesta lull but – oops – too little shaded from the sun.

* * *

'They're just experiments at this stage,' Colin said.

'Yes –?'

'Aquarelle.'

'What –?'

'Like transparent watercolours.'

He told me he wanted to see if it could suggest shadows in motion: or catch all the tiny movements – the seeming insignificances – *between the movements*. (I'm thinking of the paintings he did at Hourn, at speed, working flat-out, but

[146]

sometimes not quickly enough to avoid a shower of rain. He's running for cover, while he's trying to protect his picture from the rain, holding it paint-side down over his head.)

Aquarelle, he discovered, gave objects an even more spectral quality than gouache.

He couldn't sharpen his palette. The approximate, stone-washed colours had the feeling of memory about them, memory and dream. Life had already been lived, I felt, and this was as much as remained.

In aquarelle the woman – the person – can only be an accident of the paint.

Chance will never record her the same way twice.

I've become a passage of denser light through the palette of blues and greens. I have no shape, no outline, no profile. I have no personality, no identity of any kind.

Colin shows me the paintings. I can't think what to say, I don't say anything.

After that, he leaves the pictures for me to see or not see.

He doesn't ask me for an opinion.

I hate her.

I hate not being able to tell Colin back that no, no, this *isn't* me, and it never has been. But she persists, like a stain, like a soak mark: there and not there, and completely featureless now.

I open the copy of *Madame Bovary* in the house.

She, too, is an absence, everyone else's collusion. She pores over maps, walks down streets in her imagination, forgetting that she has already vanished.

* * *

At night my mother reappears in my dreams. She's dressed for Princes Street. She's dressed for the Saturday excursions to Barnton. She stands waiting for me at the front door of the house, growing more impatient, bag in one hand and gloves slapping against her leg.

I don't want people to call in on us any more.

I've been brought up to suppose that nothing matters more than maintaining a front. But now I can't face the bother of filtering coffee or washing and chopping a salad, and then the deadly effort of keeping bright for them.

I wait for Colin to win me round. But he seems to see that I mean what I say – I just don't feel up to another session of enforced hospitality – and he doesn't argue the point with me.

He's never raised his voice at me, he's never been tempted to lay a hand on me even when I was being difficult.

I know when I'm making things awkward. I know, and I can't stop myself. He looks on, disappointed and puzzled and – the shaming thing – full of concern for me.

Now finally the woman is outside the frame, and what's left on the canvas is the shadow she casts. Literally, the shadow.

To begin with, it takes a feminine shape. Then it becomes de-sexed. Finally it's lengthened, like a cartoon shadow run over several times by a steamroller.

* * *

The girl who serves in the bar is the owner's niece. She comes from a city, you can tell that. She looks a little bored, even in front of the customers, and definitely superior to us all.

I watch Colin watching her.

We come to this café now because he says he prefers *this* crowd to the other, although we mix with neither.

Heads turn as the girl clears the tables, in her languid manner and without any show of willingness. She reminds me of some implacable deity reincarnated; supplicated to, she is indifferent with the proto-sternness of her kind. They can petition her all they want with their eyes, but she will offer no promise of mercy.

The dazzle wears me down some days, most days, the dazzle not the heat. My own eyes were made for the muted, veiled light of the north, and now they hurt from the constant surfeit of glare.

I want to be out of the sun, which means indoors.

I feel great swathes of time are passing me by.

In Edinburgh Morven and Ailsa do their wifely duties, and are rewarded. It seems to me that my own purpose in life is a mystery. One day it may be revealed to me. In the meantime I have to carry on, with my fate unexplained.

I don't want to help deal with the pictures any more. It would mean corroborating in the process of *painting me out*.

I am not going to acknowledge what isn't going to acknowledge me.

A girl works in the dairy. She keeps out of the sun in that permanently damp and dripping cavern of a shop, blinking out at the sunlight in the street. Her strong arms are pale from carrying cheese; there's a crust of crumbly Bouignette or Crottin de Chavignon on the tips of her fingers. She wears a crisp white overall, which exposes a very exact 'V' of unblemished white skin on her chest.

She bothers me with her curds-and-whey complexion and her creamy voice as she repeats an order, blinking towards the light, and stepping back as if she's momentarily been blinded.

We have the cove to ourselves.

I go swimming, out to where the inlet becomes open sea. I find cooler water there, and the currents run faster.

I hear Colin calling me back. I wait until I'm ready to return, which has to be the moment of *my* choosing. I swim into the cove turned over on my back, so I don't have to signal across to him with my arm. I want everything to be purely instinctive.

The tin table. A pile of beans still to be split and shelled. A book, Jean Giono, turned over face-down. A pencil stub; a used white envelope with the name and address scratched out and the start of a shopping list.

At one time this raw material would have been transformed into a painting.

But now Colin works indoors. Or he goes off for walks, where I feel I would be a drag on his thoughts; he says the exercise sharpens his mind in the trough of mid-afternoon, so I tell him I'll stay here instead, in the kitchen or the garden.

Until he returns I replay that car drive from Hyères over and over in my mind. This time, though, we don't take that left-hand fork on the road which leads on to the long wooded chicane downhill to Cassis in its sheltered bay. Instead we continue up on the level, making inland, following the road signs which all bear the same poetic-sounding destination – desideratum – AIX.

She's either a waitress or a chambermaid at the hotel on the bend of road. She has her raven-black hair piled up,

which reveals her long slender neck. She walks with a
perfectly straight back, at a sedate pace which never varies.

She walks down to the town by the steps, over the rocks.
She wears sandals, with bare legs and feet. Her wide skirt
fills with breeze and lifts around her knees, giving a glimpse
of thigh.

Nothing is fixed or definite, but hazy and imprecise.

The reality is seeping out of things, in blots and blurs on
the paper. Existence seems to be running for the margin,
fleeing.

'He'.
The pronoun. 'He', 'him', 'his'.
(It's the only way to write about our life together.)
He was always further away from me than he thought he
was. The distance between us might have been feet and
inches, but really it was lines of longitude and latitude.

CHAPTER EIGHT

The Golden Isles

C olin suggested, what if I were to buy some of his
materials for him?

I'd have to do it in Marseille, I said.

Would I mind that? he asked. Some time I was going
there –

What if I made a mistake, got the order muddled up?

He said, the results might be interesting. Live and learn,
Eilidh.

I realised he wanted me away, and the business of the
materials provided him with an excuse.

I should have refused, told him no. Definitely not. But
after a couple of beats I had my answer ready for him.

Yes. All right, then.

(Momentarily I was back on the train leaving Paris, the
wheels clack-clackety-clacking on the tracks . . . the poplar
shadows falling like temple columns . . .)

Paper. An order list for canvases. A couple of soft brushes.
Some crayons. Tubes of Mars red, titanium white, and –
with a question mark placed alongside – permanent violet.

Marseille. This psychotic city, with its grand avenues and
white basilicas and acres of wretched slums. Souk stalls, the
stink of fish guts, and the glamour of distance as ships come
and go. Hundreds of thousands of people in motion,
wearing imitation-chic and burnouses; the din of unceasing
traffic; every sense assailed; and, over it all, the transform-

ing sheen of the south, gilding the mundane with something like grace.

He was right. If anything might revive me, it would be Marseille.

I found a cinema. They were showing a short season of Antonioni films.

L' Avventura, from a few years ago. The publicity stills showed a svelte, beautiful, expressionless young woman wandering about in deserted, sun-strafed de Chirico locations.

I watched the story of a socialite's disappearance turn into a performance of ennui by the rich set of casual fast-livers she came from. But it was plain boredom which afflicted some of the audience, and seats continually tipped up during the second half.

I stayed the course, somehow held by the earnest point-lessness of those lives, the elegant but throw-away conversations, the seductive views of Sicilian coastline and sea, the white yacht. The huge faces up on the screen, burdened by their beauty, were like masks; the actors' actions were a kind of mime. Automata of vague desire, and chillingly forgetful.

Outside on the street I heard a man's voice at my shoulder. A question in French.

What had I thought of the film?

It was difficult, I said.

A difficult film? Or difficult to make up my mind?

The two were connected, I told him, aware that I shouldn't have been answering a stranger's questions. I said, I didn't like obscurity for its own sake.

Did I think life was inexplicable and random like that? he asked.

Here we were talking like people in a film, I replied, and something made me laugh.

But you haven't answered my question, he persisted.

What if there isn't an answer, I was thinking to myself.

A businessman.

A charcoal-grey suit, white shirt, neatly knotted tie. Tidy short hair, combed back. Clean hands and fingernails, a faint trace of recent soap blending with the hot afternoon odour of his excitement.

A narrow sharp nose, thin straight lips: towards the priestly. And pinched eyes, with shadows beneath, some hidden emotion.

We went to a café, a glass and chrome interior near the harbour. He was in the city on business, he said. He'd had a couple of hours left over. *L' Avventura* happened to be the film they were showing, Monica Vitti was in it, and so . . .

'And you happened to find *me* to give you an opinion?'

'I was watching you in the cinema.'

Ah.

A little less random, a little less like chance. The skin of his face was drawn slightly tauter.

Two coffees.

He inhaled on his cigarette, and narrowed his eyes against the blue smoke.

The smell of smoke: I recognised it, of course. Gitanes, which Johnnie Melrose was partial to. I suffered the sting in my eyes very willingly. Again my stomach shrank, and my heart was somewhere up about my throat, just as it used to be.

Along with the coffees, two cognacs.

He didn't have to be home until later.

Dinner? he suggested.

I shook my head.

'Would you go to bed with me?' he asked.

I looked towards the window; my eyes filled with that sea light. I wasn't seeing what was there, and my eyes started to ache. I blinked down at the white formica table-top.

He was still waiting for his answer. He asked me honestly, I felt. There was something charming as well as shocking about his directness.

I heard a voice, in her Edinburgh-accented French, telling him 'Very well. Why not?'

Maybe it was Antonioni to blame. Or the memory of an afternoon long ago and far away, after I had eaten lobster and drunk Loire Muscadet.

I was thinking of the villa in Cassis with its chalet roof. I thought of the paintings I couldn't look at any longer, I thought of the piano with its lid closed and the wires untuned. I thought of my husband wanting me away.

Unconsciously I was thinking that by re-enacting a past happening – ceremonising it – maybe it was possible to help kill it, dousing it to death in its reflection.

His hands moved over me expertly. One hand from this direction, the other from that. They set up a rhythm of desire inside me.

My body bucked, writhed, jerked, as if I had no control over it. He had me at the end of a velvet rope. I was in amazement at myself, at my receptivity.

Sensations so intense I couldn't tell if they were pleasure or pain shuddered through me, from head to foot. I couldn't speak, my voice came out as gasps and groans, then as a single ecstatic scream which I turned away from him, which I emptied into the deep white fugue of pillow.

*

When? he wanted to know afterwards.

When? I repeated.

When can I see you again?

The new question swooped on me by surprise. I hadn't anticipated it. I hadn't been able to think beyond what was happening.

Next Wednesday? he asked.

'That depends.'

Would I try? he asked.

When Colin enquired I lied on the spot.

I told him that I'd left them on the train, the bits and pieces he'd wanted me to buy for him.

'I'm so sorry, what on earth was I thinking of –?'

(The moral of my immorality: get your story worked out beforehand.)

'It doesn't matter, Eilidh.'

I kept talking. I told him I'd gone to one of the shops he mentioned, they asked me to come back later, I'd been putting off half-an-hour at the harbourside, sitting outside a café, Marseille has so many cafés. And you know how you start to lose all track of time, the first hour passes . . .

He nodded his head. He smiled. He lit a cigarette, one of those menthol substitutes, and returned the carton to the cuff of his pullover. I wondered if he was really listening to me properly, he seemed only half here and half somewhere else entirely.

I told him I was hot. Go and change, he suggested, run a bath, have a long soak in the tub, I would if I were you –

In the bathroom I was immediately above his working place. He could hear my movements on the floorboards before and after, and the violent jolting of pipes as I topped up with warm water, maybe the careless slop whenever I changed position and water sluiced down the overflow between the taps.

I wasn't thinking of everything I ought to have been thinking about, I was blanking it all out. I was blanking it all out. All out.

I closed my eyes and listened to the sheer intensity of silence in the house. I held my breath and knew that in the room underneath me Colin wasn't working at all, he was holding his breath every bit as keenly as I was.

* * *

The following Wednesday I took fright. But on the Wednesday after that I was ready, nothing would have held me back from taking that risk.

He smelt of tobacco, spirits, his flannel suit. He smelt of long ago's.

I undressed slowly – because, *he* thought, I wanted to arouse him, but really because I couldn't get my mind hitched to the task. He supposed I was no novice, and he found that was exciting him.

'Wait a minute!'

There was a small commotion at the back of the room and he came across holding a glass of cognac. Somehow that made the business easier; I had a sense of inevitability now, of an event that was destined to take place.

Before the first time, and the second, and the times that followed, Colin wrote me out a shopping list.

Paper. Canvases, to be sent separately. A brush or two. Crayons, and then more particularly paints, by which shade of colour, with or without the maker's name.

Any item that had been out of stock before carried a question mark beside it.

[157]

I would recite the list to Colin as a kind of superstition, always ending with that final question mark, amplifying the contraction 'perm' to the full 'permanent' and experiencing the same little burst of imaginary violet inside my head.

* * *

I took the train up to Marseille every second Wednesday afternoon.

The notion of 'bourgeois regularity' amused me. It made the business as unexceptional as buying bread, as commonplace as shelling beans or turning the wringer handle.

I forgot that I had started to think of those Cassis tasks, on my bad days, as rituals of humiliation.

We would rendezvous in a café, the same café on the cours Franklin Roosevelt, for a fortifying drink. Then a brief walk along the rue Saint-Savournin, weaving between the other pedestrians, just another couple and yet not quite.

To the hotel, the same hotel. Past the receptionist, who had to acknowledge our custom but pretend she didn't know the nature of it. Afterwards, a phone call downstairs, and the same order despatched: tea for me, with fresh milk, and coffee for him. Dressed again, we would sit, as if *this* was the innocuous point of these encounters, the tea and the coffee, and the polite conversation staked out with pauses.

As if I was burying the memory of that first and original afternoon at the North British Hotel, the paradigm, under a surfeit of other afternoons.

Can Colin possibly suspect?

No, he doesn't know. He wouldn't smile as he does if he knew. Wide prodigal smiles.

[158]

Why so generous, unless I'm to be consoled, because he bears some shame of his own?

I study my husband closely. Can guilt identify guilt?

We watch one another, to see who will look away first.

I-Spy.

I discover my lover has a wife. A daughter. A terrier dog. He represents a firm of printers. At home they have green-striped wallpaper in their dining-room, and a pattern of acanthus leaves – red on gold – in the little salon. He drives a company car, a Panhard. His feet are size 43. He likes listening to samba. He doesn't care for gardening.

His Christian name is Alain. He doesn't tell me his surname, just as I don't tell him mine.

'Eilidh.'

I want to hear him speak my name into my ear, I want to feel his teethmarks on my shoulder, I want the rough ride back into life, as if my heart has stopped beating and needs jumpleads to start it up again. Maybe he will remind me of who I am.

Walking back up the boulevard d'Athènes, the left turn, the sweep of steps to the concourse of gare Saint-Charles, ignoring all the sly eyes that trail any single woman.

I take the slow train back. Marseille continues for miles: the fascist vistas, the North African ghettoes. During the hour or so it takes to proceed along the coast, what assurance I had when I first left the hotel peters out.

At journey's end I get down on to the station platform, fiery from the slowly sinking sun through the glass and thinking I must smell of sex. I'm sore now as I walk, but that painful sensation of chafing at the fork between my legs is proof of something, if only just that I can leave Cassis for several hours and damn to hell the consequences.

Back in the house, I have the heat of the city still on my face. I fan the air in front of me, loosen a little the disguising scarf on my neck. Whew, you could have fried an egg on the pavement, I tell Colin. He nods, and smiles in that same approximate way he has where my Wednesdays are concerned. It's *I* who try to engage *his* eyes now, but he looks away, and I'm glad to have some space around me to think in, to try to catch my thoughts.

* * *

From the back of a café on the Canabière I ring Cassis. I wait for Colin to answer. I give him the time he needs to lay aside his brush and wipe his hands and make his way through to the hall.

There is no answer.

I put down the receiver and dial again. I hear the ringing tone. I let it ring for two minutes. Three minutes.

No reply.

Either he doesn't care to answer, or he isn't there.

I replace the receiver on the cradle.

Walking out of the café I smile at the 'patron', a careless and bleary no-hope-left smile.

It's as if by being with this man, I'm trying to convince myself that the deed of adultery – like marriage – is so easily done, it's almost insignificant. This is a game, a charade, a parade of gestures.

He still doesn't know my full name, or my real identity. I doubt if he is altogether who he tells me he is.

Roles, masks. Even the words we speak are like lines

remembered from films, which were only make-believe anyway.

On a book barrow in the Cassis market I find a single volume of Proust. I buy it.

In the garden, under our magnolia tree, I slowly read about Mademoiselle Vinteuil's 'desecration' of her father's photograph. I can't translate in every detail, and it isn't stated what form the 'desecration' takes (spitting? flashing? pissing?), but, oh, I get the gist of it.

I see very clearly the truth as it applies to myself.

What else have I been trying to do in Marseille but this: abuse and punish the image of my mother which I carry. I'm trying to tell her, because I have done it too, *your* affair hasn't meant a thing. Adultery is within everyone's reach. Mine, Colin's, yours, Johnnie Melrose's. It passes the afternoon, it puts in the empty time. There's no skill or talent involved, see, except in deceiving: and if, chère maman, if you suppose this amounts to more than the smallness of its tawdry parts, then you were only deceiving yourself all along.

But I couldn't do to my mother what was done to Monsieur Vinteuil. She refused to play this game of literary replication.

This was one situation which wouldn't be rationalised. I couldn't neatly work in parallels and paradigms, expecting my psychological equations to balance obligingly.

The dead are safe. They have their secrets. Whenever I thought about Lindsey Guthrie, when I closed my eyes to catch a sight of her, she was still defiantly smiling back at me.

Her smile turns to velvety laughter as the car travels downhill. She laughs at the distance ahead, at the road pitching and rolling on its descent to Dawyck and the valley floor, to where the silvery Tweed sedately curves and meanders.

The car is gathering speed all the time. The sheep cropping in the fields raise their heads, stare. Peewits and plovers skim overhead. The clouds in the sky are high and fleecy and tranquil.

Laughter seems the only response to make to the situation, to this late-afternoon delight. It's not an escape, but rather it's a release.

My mother feels as if bubbles of air have entered her bloodstream. Her head is featherlight, and when she realises *how* light she laughs again. She fills her eyes with the radiance of the day, with its lavish blaze. The sheep go scattering; the darting birds flit low across the fields. The car's radiator devours the red road. The sun spins along the top of the windshield.

My mother glows with the imperturbable confidence of someone who is certain she is truly loved.

* * *

'You're back, Eilidh.'

He always says it, Colin, and he always sounds surprised. As if one time I might *not* return.

I show him what I've managed to buy from the shopping list.

'I still can't find any permanent violet.'

'I'm out of that one. I wonder if you can still get it.'

He could ask me to place an order, I'm thinking.

'Is it different from the other violets?'

'They lose their brilliance,' he says.

'I'll keep looking.'

'Don't worry about it too much.'

One afternoon I tried three different shops. The

supplier's where I do all my buying now has nothing of that description.

'I'm sorry.'

'Maybe next time,' Colin says.

In another fortnight's time it concludes the list again. The question mark is a fixture.

? perm. violet

Whether or not the paint exists, it functions as a kind of totem, my lucky charm.

Lucky?

I call Cassis again from a phone booth at the station. I give Colin time to reach the phone.

No answer.

I replace the receiver, then pick it up and dial again. I stand with the receiver to my ear while a waiting couple ostentatiously pace the pavement outside.

'I rang you,' I say when I get back.

'When?'

'In the middle of the afternoon.'

'I didn't hear, I'm afraid.'

'I thought you must be out,' I told him.

'I could have been.'

'You went out?'

'Yes. Or you might have got the wrong number.'

'I redialled.'

'Could be something wrong with the connections.'

My conscience isn't as muddied as it might be.

Why wasn't he there to answer the phone when I rang him?

Too busy painting?

No.

Where is the evidence of myself in those paintings? My 'I' is being refused a real life.

So, why should it matter, what happens every second Wednesday, once the train pulls out of the little station and takes me off?

In the hotel, with the windows closed and curtain drawn, Alain and I could be anywhere. The sounds of Marseille fall away, and what's left is the occasional thunder-roll of the plumbing. What's left is the breath coming out of him and out of me, but not beating in time.

? perm. violet

I see the words in technicolor violet, I *hear* them like a slow bass under my breathing.

'Per-man-*ent* vi-o-*let*. Per-man-*ent* vi-o-*let*.'

He, Alain, might be anyone. Once upon a time I thought I caught a resemblance to Struan Melrose, who reminded me of someone else, but I can't see it now, not for the life of me.

* * *

HM the Queen will confer the knighthood on him at Holyrood Palace. How our mother would have loved to be Lady Guthrie! – having the harridans serving in the shops bow and scrape to her. *She* had a part in our father's success, but what fate gives with one hand it takes away with the other. So, it will just be him on his own, altho' Alasdair and I will be at the investiture, and Ailsa with her Ming if they aren't off on their travels at the time. *Sir* Ranald Guthrie – we'll all need to get used to that!

I shall pass on to him your congratulations, shall I? –
unless you would prefer to do it personally? Let me
presume you would prefer the former.

* * *

Our Marseille affair finished, because the sex wasn't suffi-
cient by itself and because I couldn't think where we might
be heading. I couldn't remember any more why it should be
more urgent than anything else to be there for him at a
certain time on a certain day. I was an actress who had
forgotten the lines of the script . . .

One Wednesday I got off the train at Saint-Charles and
crossed the concourse to another platform and got on to a
Toulon train heading back the way I'd just come. I wondered what I was going to say to Colin about not having
bought any of the materials on my shopping list. I could
blame the hot day, blame something I'd eaten yesterday,
blame that elusive permanent violet which no shop stocked.

Back in Cassis, I saw him out walking, my husband, a
tiny figure clambering over the rubble of rocks that led out
along the headland.

I spent the afternoon in the kitchen, never far from the
back door. I vaguely imagined what must be happening. An
empty place at our table in the café. The hotel receptionist
would be shaking her head again. 'Still no message,
M'sieur.' The tea and the coffee wouldn't be arriving on
the porter's tray.

I had no regrets. To do so, I would have needed to *be in
love* with my lover. Or he with me.

'Lover' was just a lazy word, applied to someone who
probably didn't have the first idea what it might mean.

Next time, or the one following, my place would be
occupied again; a couple would join the crowds on the

cours Franklin Roosevelt, the rue Saint-Savournin; the receptionist would consult the register as if their arrival was a surprise to her; the order phoned downstairs would be for a pot of coffee for two to be sent up.

The role had been mine to play for a while, but now it was another's.

* * *

'Quick about,
And then away,
Lightly dance
The glad Strathspey.'

I try to catch the movement of day into night, but I never can.

When I'm unable to sleep I get up and watch the sky for night's end. The French talk of the green ray, which is the first notification of day. I see no ray, of any colour, and by the time I realise the sky is finally lightening I've missed the changeover.

I hack away at the bushes in the garden. (There's too much shade; I want openness, clarity.) But over the decades they've grown long complicated roots. They're more stubborn than the cacti, quite impossible to dig up; they cling to life ferociously every time I try, I get nowhere with them.

'Slowly, smiling,
As in France,
Follow through
The country dance.'

I decide to grow my nails, longer than they already are.

With talons I won't any longer be a woman who keeps house or who gardens.

I tell Colin to apologise to the colonel for me. Next time, I say, I shall feel better.

'What *are* you feeling, Eilidh?'

I make a face.

He announces he won't go either in that case.

'But you must, Colin,' I'm answering back. 'Or the old boy'll drop us, and that'll be the end of our social life in Cassis.'

By the time they were opening their first bottle, I was at the Saint-Charles station. I got a train from there to Aix.

A small hotel, in a leafy square with a fountain. The Old Town is a warren of narrow lanes, one person wide in places. High buttressed walls, and tiny deep-set windows with grilles. Caryatids valiantly struggle to support crumbling palaces.

In my room I find a radiator just like the one in the painting, curled round and round on itself like a serpent.

I come across a museum of Provencal life. Or rather, Provençal death.

I examine the procession of dusty wooden figures extended over three glass cases. Mounted bishops and altar boys, sepulchral madonnas and painted whores, devils on horseback, seigneurs in litters, Jews in chains being goaded with sticks, prancing red cats.

Lords of misrule. The world has been subverted, somersaulted upside-down, it has *become* its own reflection.

*

SHE is walking down a long street, the rue Mignet, carrying a suitcase.

Someone calls out to HER. HER name, twice.

SHE recognises the name, and stops.

The little blue Gordini is parked on the corner, by the opposite pavement. My husband gets out. He stands looking, raises his arm slowly, opens his hand in a silent wave.

The people of Aix hurry past.

Neither of us moves for several moments; we're as still as statues.

'I've come to take you home, Eilidh.'

He takes my case from me.

I follow him across the little square. I get into the car and he closes the door after me.

We drive off, not speaking.

He steers the car carefully through the streets. We reach the outskirts of the town; he can pick up speed now.

Air blows in through the side windows.

We don't talk about what has happened.

Back at the house, back at 'La Croix du Sud', still nothing is said about the missing days.

Colin takes the suitcase upstairs. I wonder all the while if I'm going to scream the walls down or if he's going to lift his hand to me for the first time.

But the minutes pass. He makes some coffee for us. Too much chicory, but we drink it, grateful for something to do, we're as ready for it as we once were for the coffee at the Brasserie Lipp or at Maigret's favourite Café Ma Bourgogne over in the Marais.

I don't want to look at myself in the mirror, in case I lose this frail sense of composure. I don't look at anything too closely, to put off recognising it a little longer, until I can be calmer.

[L'ALLÉE BLANCHE]
I can give you the details. Oh yes.

Where. That narrow lane in Cassis. The patch of wall. Which tree's shadow spikes the broken plasterwork.

When. The calendar date, the time of day, what we were doing before and after.

But it doesn't explain everything, or anything.

Not why.

Not how.

Colin painted what appears to be a moment in time, random and accidental.

The painting occupied him for several days. The moment – that emptiness on the square of canvas – lasted eight days.

Although I was gone, he didn't stop painting. His work kept him together, in one piece. I had helped to give him that much assurance; it was his link to me. So long as he painted, he knew I would come back to him.

The green ray. No, a false dawn.

Finally I haven't any means of resisting. There is no 'in spite of myself'.

The past is luring me back, I feel, with that mass – that mess – of unfinished business.

> *'O such a hurry-burry!*
> *O such a din!*
> *O such a hurry-burry*
> *Our house is in!'*

* * *

[THEREFORE I AM]

A country road.

Two long black straight lines fall forward in broadening perspective. They're the shadows of someone's legs.

A tiny ant-like body on top, at the far end.

The picture is semi-stylised. It's not an identifiable road, and the legs are generic.

From our arrival this was a land of shadows, of contrasts. But now the 'I', 'me', 'mine' have been fully transferred from the substance to the projection.

Water down a plughole, spinning clockwise down
down
down

Through levels of transparency the past in plenty comes shining back at me. I get vertigo, I can't bear to look and yet I'm fascinated to see all that way down, into the deeps. There seems to be nothing separating me, no protection; I could lose my balance and go tumbling head over heels, arsy-versy.

I paint my hands.

I paint them blue.

Blue. Not violet, but hyacinth blue.

I varnish my long nails green. Apple-green.

I should get up and go, I should leave for good. For good or for bad. But I don't.

I need to be surer of myself for that. I need to believe the journey is worth making, and that there's something better ahead of me. More than that I need to believe in Eilidh Brogan as someone who's quite sure of herself, who's hard-edged and definite (a bit like the rocks where Colin takes his solitary walks) but that is impossible.

Langoustes.

They served langoustes in Rogano's. One lunchtime, long ago.

It isn't the taste I recognise; before that, it's the weight of shell on the plate, the way one pincer hangs over the side with such sang-froid, such world-weariness, and the instantaneous smell of wide sea.

> *'Hey den dilly dow,*
> *How dan den.'*

* * *

My mother returned, briefly.

One evening I found her on the staircase, at the darkest part.

Another day, early one morning, she was in the garden, standing beneath the magnolia tree.

How had she found me?

And why now?

The first time I slammed a door on her. The second time I ran back into the house and upstairs and locked myself in the bathroom.

Death, I felt, was in the air. It had puts its claim on this house, too, and on its garden.

What did she know, and why did she bring this memento mori to us now?

I dreamed I had taken a book to read in the garden. I opened it and found the pages were numbered but blank, the text was missing. As I leafed through the pages, the spine of the book cracked and split; in slow motion the pages came loose and fanned as I tried to catch them, before they ended up scattering in all directions.

Everything was a symbol, as Proust says, and every symbol bore a message.

All those portents were mocking me, for being the very last to know.

I had run away from Paris without a second thought. The future could look after itself; present time was enough to be getting on with.

I had got further from Paris than I could have supposed. Sometimes it felt too far to ever make my way back.

Colonnaded gardens with a bench, and gardeners laying the dust.

A café, with an empty table in the corner, and sun slanting through the window at a certain angle.

The Embarkation for Cythera, which was really a return.

I was dry between my legs.

A parched place. A desert land.

It hurt me even when Colin explored, spread his hand and covered me with his fingers. Any more than that and I started to burn.

I tried to explain to him. He asked me if I might not be imagining it to be worse than it was: imagining it in the first place, I presumed he meant, making it up.

'What if we found a doctor for you?'

'And tell him what?'

How could I have let a doctor examine what I was so reluctant to let my husband see?

'Maybe it'll clear up by itself,' I said. 'It just needs time.'

The skin between my legs was red and flaky; I wore my rawness like a badge, and no one could have been in any doubt.

'It's all right, Eilidh.'

He's endlessly patient, and I can't abide it. I want him to shout at me, to call me the worst names he can think of.

I deserve no respect at all.

I deserve nothing.

If we hadn't met in Paris, if he had left things as we'd left them at Hourn, maybe I would have got better in my head. Or maybe I would have had another breakdown. But it wouldn't have been like this.

I could try, try to go back to Paris, try to lose myself in all that blue light.

Colin goes to the studio and gets on with his work.

He keeps away for three, four, five hours, however many he needs.

Then I feel I'm at the bottom of a black hole, I'm in a pit, or I'm in the lightless deep deeps of the sea.

I've managed to forget the *point* of playing the piano.

How bourgeois. For salon entertainment. Music to distract from the passing of time. Music to dream your life away to.

* * *

Colin is talking about the Îles d'Or again.

We've put it off and put it off.

We should go, he says, we must go. To Porquerolles or

[173]

Port-Cros. It's as if he anticipates we won't be here much longer. We must go and see them now.

The folklore of the Scottish Highlands has it that the Isles of the Blest – Paradise, by another name – lies over the horizon: just over there, on the other side of that thin dividing line.

At Hyères the ferry was waiting.

'Ready, Eilidh?'

I stared at him.

'It's all right,' he grinned back. 'I'll be sea-sick *with* you!'

He'd got that wrong, quite wrong. All those boats I used to go sailing with up at Hourn, I had grown up having sea-legs.

He took my arm and led me up the gangplank.

He had brought a sketchpad with him, for roughs and jottings. No crayons, no paints. Today was meant to be a holiday of sorts.

We had talked about coming for four years. Now we were almost there. I felt nothing about it.

I sat down on one of the side benches on deck. He came and sat beside me. Here I was looking neither forwards nor back but out to open sea. Far away, the first landfall must be Africa. I pictured bazaars, carpets hanging from balconies, a loaded camel at a city gate, passing through the eye of a needle.

He said something. My eyes hurt from the glare of the sea. When I turned my head I had to blink several times to see him, to get my focus. He was smiling back at me, disclaiming my seriousness.

There was a very *actual* smell of oil and garlic and cheap cigarettes.

He found an elastic band to put round the sketchbook,

to stop the pages fluttering. I watched his small, meticulous attention, the precise stoop of his neck, the drop of his head.

I turned back to the sea, I looked for the horizon. But the sea and the sky were one. Out there somewhere was Africa, and a new beginning.

* * *

I can smell pine even before we reach Port-Cros. The ancient balm of the trees, from a thousand years ago.

The island isn't golden, but green and blue on saffron scored with white. Sea laps on to sheer rocks. There's sand, caves.

Colin is standing by my side at the railing, he does the talking for both of us. I'm not really listening, he can do the thinking for me too, my head is still taken up with Africa.

We proceed in a kind of trance.

The day has the inevitability of something dreamed.

I'm not surprised by what I see on the long walk through Solitude Valley, although it's entirely new to me.

The eagles overheard. Springs of pristine clear water burbling from rock.

Rosemary crushed underfoot. Yellow broom, and purple heather ablaze.

The clifftop path. A mountain called Vinaigre. Another valley called La Fausse Monnaie, 'false currency'.

Colin takes my arm. Another uphill, downhill track, which carries us between banks of eucalyptus and wild geraniums. The air smells overpoweringly sweet.

He hopes I'm not tiring myself, and I can see what he's thinking, that maybe even now two can turn into three. He holds me again; I have to tell him if I want to rest, don't talk if I don't want to. Just enjoy the day, admire the splendours.

> *'Here we go round the jing-a-ring,*
> *Jing-a-ring, jing-a-ring.'*

The other visitors have gone on their way. We're alone with the trees and the birdsong and now and then the flurry of butterflies drawn to the brilliant red of the rampant jacarandas.

The sun is at its zenith, roaring down at us where the trees have thinned out. We've been walking for too long to remember. I feel my legs are working by clockwork.

> *'Here we go round the jing-a-ring,*
> *About the merry matenzie.'*

My head is at boiling point from the sun. A pain splits it from one side to the other. Colin tells me I'm not looking like myself. And when I start laughing, mirthlessly to my ear, he says I should get some rest in the shade.

I nod down at the sea. I can cool off there, it occurs to me, I can swim away from my troubles.

He leads the way down a steep path, past cork oaks. We slide and slither, and steer ourselves by grabbing hold of the hardy gorse bushes with their thorn stems. My hands are stinging from them; the backs of my legs hurt just as badly from the grit I keep skidding on. Several of my long nails splinter.

We scramble down on to a shingle strand. It's a cove we don't know, we've never set eyes on it before, but it's an archetypal cove nevertheless, the one we're destined to come across.

The limestone cliffs hide us. I slip into my swimsuit.

I leave Colin and walk into the water. I don't tell him to follow. He's sitting with his sketchpad open, to record his initial impressions. Forget art, I want to say, to hell with the living moment frozen in time –

I swim out to deeper water.

Cooler currents pulse beneath the calm surface, mysteriously disturbing the water layers beneath. Then weed shifts, and sunshine floods the inlet with light, and the hazard just as mysteriously disappears, or seems to.

I swim past such treacherous bounty. Watch long enough and you would see only a perfect stillness. But the bay is a battleground. It's as if the rocks cling to primeval grudges, while the sunlight of Phoenicians and Greeks and Romans continually seduces –

I would like to go on swimming, nothing else, even though I can already hear Colin's voice calling. Right out to open sea and on and on, and discover if the horizon ever comes any closer. Through submerged cathedrals and the ruins of sunken cities, and on and on and never come back. I have nothing to come back *to*, nobody – no 'me' – I have to be or I can believe in any more.

I need more strength than I've got. My head still hurts. Another day. Or evening might be better still, in the cool air, and the moon lays a shining path for me to follow, into the temple of the night. Until I reach the green ray, and pierce dawn, the new day.

I swim back, and haul myself up the ramp of shingle on my hands and knees. My head is spinning. Three into two won't go anyway.

Colin sits up on a rock sketching. He calls down, but I sink my hands into the weight of pebbles; oceans pulverise in the swell of sound.

Rrrrssh.

I turn away and clamber to my feet. On the rocks opposite his perch, I see footholds. I slowly pick my way up. A pine tree on the cliffside throws some shadow, and I roll under its blueness.

Cicadas trill somewhere. A branch creaks up in the tree, like a ship's timber. A lolling giant sighs from the shingle shore.

I lie flat against the dark rock. I want only coolness, shade. My head hurts too much to think; I feel it go flichtering off. I spread my arms and legs, finding hollows and bumps in the rock to accommodate me. I make a stone wedding. Nothing comes between us, no cause or impediment.

I lie in a position Colin has painted me in several times before. I am aware that he is in the water, but I'm not listening for him.

My head is held by a single string, too light for any thoughts at all. All the sounds of the day pass through me, and I forget, I lose consciousness.

Something wakes me. A cry.

Who can that . . .

I lie on the rock with one ear uncovered.

Again.

A name.

'Eilidh!'

I turn my head, look round.

There used to be a time when Colin called it out in our lovemaking, just like that, as if in surprise.

Why now?

When I get there, he's looking up at me from beneath the water. It's how he looked at me when I tried teaching him to swim at first, in the cold Atlantic. His brown eyes are pleading with me to help.

Show me what to do!

But I can't move. I'm weighted to the spot. I'm rock.

'Eilidh!'

Why *that* name? The voice is odd, rippling round a crag, a strange voice calling to a stranger.

'Eilidh, please!'

My reality is in the water. Outside the water, doesn't he understand, I cease to have any. It's been like this for weeks, months, years maybe.

I'm no one. He's made me a nobody. I don't exist in the paintings. A figure in the carpet, worked into the design, a smudge or a smear, a shadow falling.

I watch my shadow on the water, passing across him.

There's nobody here to help him, to show him what to do.

Mourn for her, weep for her. Plead all you will, but she's gone, she's lost.

His eyes close, open again.

Seconds pass, or minutes.

His face as it recedes is trusting, faithful, credulous. His mouth makes a gentle and forgiving smile.

He's falling. He floats away from me. His face blurs.

His movements become calmer, and the water quietens.

I've been standing here all my life. *He* has been fated to this forever.

His hands wave above him, like an elegant farewell. Goodbye to no one.

His eyes have closed. They stay shut.

Down and down. The water rolls over him.

Sumptuous colours ripple beneath him. He's turned on his side and he seems to be caught running across a blue-green field.

The effects are dazzling, mesmerising. The sun shines in, and suddenly where the weed at a cave's mouth bleeds red and green, it radiates the one colour he could never find, the most brilliant and lustrous of violets.

Down and down he goes, to where wind blows from the caves, a cold numbing wind, and into the beckoning arms of the bloody red weed.

Such beauty, such cruelty.

Some bubbles are left scattered on the surface. Casual, inconsequential. A final scribble of signature.

CHAPTER NINE

Aller-Retour

The gendarmes spoke to me. Or they tried to extract from me what sense they could, but of course in the circumstances . . .

Phrases that wouldn't connect into meaningful sentences. Words which I could only repeat. Silences I fell into.

Morven was in the house, telling me what a sorry to-do *this* was, and no date for a funeral even, that's France for you.

She asked me what my preferences were for the funeral.

'Burial,' I said.

Then I changed my mind. 'Cremation'.

'Cremation?'

I changed my mind again. 'No, burial.'

Morven asked me, was I sure? I said I *wasn't* sure.

'Well, we can't go on like this.'

Buried where? Scotland, which he had left for my sake? No.

Our garden? Or a lair in the shade of pine trees, beside the sea?

Places to haunt.

'No,' I said. 'No. Not burial.'

'Cremation, then?'

I nodded.

'And that's your final word, Eilidh?'

I didn't say anything, and so Morven must have supposed that it was.

*

There were phone calls, with the door kept shut so I shouldn't hear. I had to speak to a lawyer in Edinburgh. A telegram. More phone calls for Morven. Another telegram. Official forms for this and that.

Colin James Brogan went up in smoke, into the cerulean of French sky.

His ashes were raked up, and mixed with others, and they were used to feed the soil of a farmer's field somewhere.

I couldn't even cry.

I heard Morven telling Ailsa on the phone, there had been no tears, can you believe it, none at all.

Morven let me see her eyeing my long fingernails disapprovingly.

I ought to have resisted her, but now I couldn't remember why I had grown them like this.

I clipped them. Mulberry varnish wasn't worn by widows, so I varnished them clear, like a decent Godfearing soul.

'You won't be staying on here, I suppose.'
I stared at Morven.
'Why on earth not?'
'After what's happened?'
'I've nowhere else to go.'
She hesitated.
'I presumed,' she said, 'you'd be thinking of coming back.'
'Back where?'

'To Edinburgh, of course.'

'Why should I do that?'

She narrowed her eyes to look at me. She was making neither head nor tail of my obtuseness.

'Well, it's your home, isn't it?'

'Not now,' I say.

'Not *immediately*.'

'No.'

'No what?'

'No to coming home.' I corrected myself. 'To going back there.'

'You just need some time, to think about it.'

Morven wouldn't accept that she might not be right. Even the best part of a thousand miles from *her* normality, that possibility didn't occur to her.

We left it at that. I didn't argue the point. Both of us wanted to get through these few days with the semblance of civility, as we'd all three daughters had instilled into us. The future wasn't really important now. Anyway, time was taking us further and further from one another, her and me: out of mutual harm's way if we could let enough time pass, I out of her ken and she out of mine.

* * *

I was alone in the house at last.

I was lying in our bed. I sat at the kitchen table looking at Colin's empty chair.

I thought I could still hear his footsteps. But I didn't hurry to close a door or cover my ears. If his spirit wanted to find me, it would.

*

I dreamed of the cove. But now I was on my knees reaching out a hand to him, or I was in the water diving down to where he was.

When I woke, I believed it for several moments. Then the realisation dawned. No. No, that wasn't how it had been.

Ailsa wrote, come and see us, why don't you? We'll be in London on these dates, could you manage to coincide –?

I thought about it.

But now wasn't the time to leave, with the sense of Colin's presence still about. This was where we had made our home. It was where we had belonged, and where I still belonged.

I tried to do things according to the routine we'd had.

The furniture stayed exactly where it had been. I used the same crockery, the same towels. I left the same plants and flowers in the garden, in their habitual locations.

I came back in from the garden one day and realised I was washing my hands with the same bar of soap *he* had used, and I burst into tears, my first tears, for the unattainable closeness of him.

The air in the house seemed coagulated to silence. I could imagine the mass of it pushing hard against the walls, so that they were starting to buckle outwards.

Every little single sound encased inside was magnified.

Then one day the skies opened, there was a downpour, and I was grateful for the full-throttled stour: rods of rain, rain being flung like gravel against the windows. I stared out at the garden filling with water, through the slithering rain-trails on the glass.

Grief was suddenly flooding the world. I cried, too, to be a part of it.

Across the room, in the wardrobe mirror, a woman with red eyes and older than myself stood with her mouth hanging helplessly slack. She seemed not to recognise me either, we agreed to differ, and passed in the glass.

I lay on top of the bed, in sunshine. I watched the reflections of garden vegetation on the ceiling. I listened to the chattering cicadas, the desultory noontime birdsong. I was lying here again on that first morning of heat and light, on the same bed, when everything was new and wonder-filled, when I had imagined I was starting out on my life again, and nothing left to think back on.

I took his clothes from the wardrobe and laid them out. From the cloth I could still detect him in my nostrils. I had lived with him, scarcely conscious that he had an individual smell at all. But now I could recognise it at once – soapy, mentholy, a little sweaty, musky, turpsy. I passed the material under my nose, and his presence was filling my head.

It was as if he had come back. And when I realised that, I needed to leave the room, leave the house and walk about the garden for a long time, trying to ride the storm of thoughts in my head.

* * *

Rutherford's were asking me about the paintings.

I continued to put them off.

In the end, though, I knew I would have to look at the paintings, I couldn't go on with them leaning against walls, turned away from me, and those parts of the house left in darkness.

I dreaded seeing them. But that time would have to be confronted eventually, because the pictures told all the various truths about Colin Brogan and the woman he married.

The unbearable silence of the rooms, like asphyxia.

I sat down at the piano. I lifted the lid. I watched my hands spread on the keys. I listened to the sounds that emerged from the piano's deep rumbling belly, music which I had again at the tips of my fingers.

I hadn't played for months. Now I sat and played out all that lost time. I wasn't aware of how long for until I felt a dull ache in my spine. I got up stiffly, shook pins and needles out of my arms.

Somehow, I sensed, the worst danger was past, even though it had been touch and go. No dervishing panic inside my head. No damburst of tears. I was breathing evenly, regularly. Everything was contained, just.

I went to bed, the bed Colin and I had shared. I was suddenly overcome with fatigue, and my head dropped back on to the pillow, sank into the dense weight of old duck feathers.

I fell asleep without realising. I slept through until the morning, and woke with the postman's ringing the bell on the gate in the wall.

* * *

Letters. The first of the letters, enquiries about the paintings that remained.

To begin with, only a few a week. After several months

there will be a couple of dozen a week, which each asks its questions and (politely for the most part) requests an answer.

I had put off the business of cataloguing, because of all it must uncover.

Once I'd started, though, I couldn't stop. One canvas led me to another, to another. I wracked my brain to remember all I could about the circumstances of painting. I cross-referred to the preparatory sketches Colin had made, and to his scrawled notes.

In time I shall try to trace every picture that's been sold, even the early ones that were used as barter. Meanwhile I was writing to dealers and gallery-proprietors, to owners and ex-owners. I had to be patient, hoping that they would be able to tell me what I wanted to know or that I would receive a reply at least, even if I was being told to wait.

I began with Colin's informal memos and timesheets, and referred everything back to those. The dog-eared day-by-day pocket diaries gave me my outline structure, my template.

I became immersed in that past. Coming out of it every time was like throwing off chains. But when I got back – to this other side – I was equally exhausted and bereft.

When I wasn't tracking the paintings I was playing the piano.

Some days I practised for three or four hours. I stopped noticing the passage of time; I concentrated on the music alone.

The music was perpetually itself, timeless and unchanging: beyond time and alteration.

Whichever I was doing, I ate only when I became conscious I was hungry, I drank if I realised I had a thirst. I went out for air and some exercise only when I started to feel cramp in my legs, numbness in the small of my back.

Between the music and my cataloguing, I sloughed off the mental inertia of the past weeks, months, years even.

It seemed to me that I was rediscovering myself.

And that was the terrible guilt, another abomination, which I had to acknowledge and confront.

Only a death close to us can make us feel properly alive, and revivify us.

It had taken my husband's death to restore my pulse, to send life racing back through me.

* * *

Initially, just a handful of pupils. Then, as my reputation quietly spread, more.

I didn't dissuade anyone who wanted to come. Music, I now knew, put them in touch with thoughts and feelings they might not be able to express in any other way. Music, I had learned from my own experience, liberates the trapped spirit.

They expected me to be more serious perhaps, stricter. But I had these quite altered expectations of them now.

The sounds of music – music of some description – filled the rooms of the house. At the end of the day I could still see my charges' faces and hear their voices, and so my surroundings – the inescapably familiar – became easier for me to bear.

I left what was pinned up on the studio wall. Not only the postcards and newspaper curios, but the wrappings and labels: from a tin of Portuguese sardines or Moroccan anchovies or a box of Tunisian dates, the lacey gilt paper which once lined a small carton of chocolate pralines, the luridly yellow tissue paper used by a fruiterer to protect a pomegranate.

Everything else I spread out on top of the kitchen table.
Domestic memorabilia, and my source material.
Photographs. Bills, receipts. More newspaper clippings. Recipes. Railway timetables. Letters, postcard views. Folded strips of paper for bookmarks, covered with jottings. Road-maps. Train tickets. Rough pencil sketches on used envelopes. Complimentary sachets of matches from hotels. A ferry boarding-pass. A leaflet guide to the Îles d'Or. An illustration in a school history primer, the murder of David Rizzio by jealous courtiers in front of his lover Mary Queen of Scots. Pebbles collected from various beaches, some pine cones.
The violet which never loses its violence of colour, which scalds the eye with its fury and truth, which won't fade in memory.
I was looking at it forever.

Now I understood that if any of my pupils wasn't responding properly, then the fault was mine, for not explaining, for not being able to show them that music might proclaim an enthusiasm for life.
Music is *about* life. At its most extreme, it lies at the limit of the humanly knowable; what the music *I* was teaching did was to express in a subtler language than words what it is we feel, and what it is that connects us to one another (the shared experience of this repertoire of feelings). Music smooths out and resolves the very contradictions between these *different* feelings; it orders dissonances, establishes

harmonies, unifies all the elements which originally threat-
ened to undo it.

Also this, stuck up on the studio wall.

*ONLY ART AND MEMORY ARE PROOF AGAINST THE DE-
STRUCTIVENESS OF TIME.*

We're how we were *before*. The accident is still ahead of us;
the visit to the Îles d'Or hasn't been planned yet.

Is one of us going to mention the fateful place? I can try to
stop it being said, but Colin's voice – always louder – will
talk over me, arguing the trip so persuasively.

So I sit still at the kitchen table, lying low, and maybe
what is to come will glide over my head and get spirited off
in quite another direction, and *what will be* becomes instead
what might have been, and we're rescued, we're safe.

I knew my capacities as a pianist. I didn't hanker after a
career. I was a provincial teacher of amateurs, and that was
that. There was nothing for me to regret.

It was enough that I should transmit my enjoyment of the
music to my pupils, and to encourage them to believe in
their own abilities.

I discovered – a chance remark from someone at Rutherford's – that some of the earliest paintings, purchases
recorded in the name of Kerr, had in fact been bought
by one J. W. L. Melrose of Moray Place.

I taught the piano. I was also Colin Brogan's widow.

The new life brought a trickle of visitors: dealers, a few
collectors, a gallery curator from Edinburgh followed by his
rival from Glasgow, a couple of writers from art journals, a
newspaper journalist.

I stopped seeing those people for a while. But the enquiries continued, and in the final reckoning they had to be dealt with.

* * *

A package arrived one day. It was addressed to me, with an Edinburgh frank-mark. I didn't recognise the handwriting.
I took it to the kitchen table and opened it up.
Inside a sealed envelope, a letter.

Dear Mrs Brogan,
We have never met. I should like to have had a chance to meet you, but I felt I knew a good deal about you from Colin.
    We were friends from our student days. A tragedy linked us. Now another tragedy links *us*, you and me.
    You may not know, but Colin occasionally wrote to me. I was always a kind of willing ear for him, and I wouldn't have told a soul. We were never romantically paired, if I can put it like that: just good friends. I heard about you from the very outset, from when he first went up to your holiday place at Hourn. *He* was always discreet, always unfailingly fair. I was very fond of him.
    I believe that these letters really belong to you. I think he would have wanted you to have them – that's why he was really writing them maybe – they might help clarify certain matters for you.
    These days everyone seems to be talking about his paintings, don't they? The letters belong to his reputation now, and *you* must be their custodian.
    Kind regards,
    June McMurchie

Oh, June McMurchie, I don't think I'm very convinced by you. You enter the story unbidden, at a moment when I can't do anything to stop you.

How can I trust you? Who are you exactly, tell me, and what was your relationship with the man I married?

You wait patiently, June McMurchie. Thirty minutes, an hour. For as long as it takes.

Finally, I reach into the envelope and pull out the enclosures, as she knows I shall. Against my better judgement I start to read, the first lines of the letters on top, and after that – of course – there is no going back.

If you hadn't been there, June, I'd have given up at that Guthrie stone wall – I wdn't have asked Melrose if you hadn't suggested it, & so I wdn't have known Eilidh was in Paris.

So I wdn't have gone & found her & I wdn't have had the experience of coming south & feeling I was seeing the world for the very 1st time in my life.

I've returned to oils for the southern colours – for what seems so fixed and resolute – and the stark black of the shadows (saw-edged). All these possibilities!

All the hours I spent in the Artschool rooms – oh, the tantalising smell of paraffin heat, but never enough of it, & my arms too stiffly by my sides. It seems like another life I used to have.

Eilidh settles a room around her – with a few quick gestures she imposes her system on it – it's not just any room, somehow it's been personalised.

I have never lived so intensely – consecrated by the

[192]

splendour of the sun – in this radiant seclusion. All I work to do is to illustrate MY PLEASURE & enjoyment. It's just as simple & as complicated as that.

In the window? And what does Dundas Street think as it walks past? A snapshot of our eldorado life here, amid the douce grey decencies of Edinburgh!
[Frame ok?]
Let's hope **someone** stops & thinks it's worth a 2nd look, those 11 (?) steps down from the street.
Rutherford's wd prefer recognisable **scenes**, like the Baie des Anges, or something in the garden. They'd like me to go on painting them forever. And on the profits we'd be able to hire a fast car & get ourselves up to Paris or over to London maybe. (We cd start to resemble the sort of people who buy paintings in chi-chi galleries.)
No, let's be honest – I don't see it, do you?

So, I wd have nothing to report without Eilidh.
Things compose themselves around her, in relation to her (have I said all this?), in the context of **this woman**.
If she wasn't here, the rest wd just fall away.

We talk about the Golden Isles.
It's 'our lighthouse', she says, but I don't understand, & she shakes her head at me, but not unkindly.

I feel that if I paint her I can recover her, I can fetch her back from the precipice she's drawn to. It's never done – she's pulled there time & again, to that drop, & I have to do some magic again, perform the ritual.
Atonement, salvation, I don't know what.

[193]

Aquarelle: so spinsterish-sounding somehow, & yet this is how I've rediscovered the DANGER there might be in painting. There's only so much I can plan, the rest is a matter of chance.

I read and re-read his letters. I strained to see in the gathering dark.

What had she *not* sent me?

Had she thought she could spare me worse? Worse was imagining what I didn't know, the gaps between the letters that I did have.

But worst of all, the very worst, was starting to under-stand everything I had failed to at the time, turning the story I had thought I already knew upside-down and inside-out.

Now it was the middle of the night. Moths were stuck to the window.

I felt I had lived my life through several times. I hadn't any energy left. I let my head fall on to the table.

I woke up with my face lying in a wedge of white sunlight. The old wood smelt hot; it smelt of some fabulous, imper-ishable forest.

Morning.

I had missed it again: night turning to day: the elusive, momentary green ray.

(But see the ray, even just once, and what was left in the future to steal your imagination?)

In the studio I found two unopened tubes on the top shelf of the cupboard, hidden at the back.

I read the labels.

'PERMANENT VIOLET'.

A bomb goes off inside my head. In the stunned aftermath everything falls back down to earth, but settling in a different order.

They're among other tubes which I did bring back from Marseille. He couldn't have forgotten about them, they were part of his store of oils, from some previous batch he'd bought by himself.

'I'm out of that one,' he would say to me.

Always the list in pencil, and – last entry of all – *perm violet* accompanied by its question mark.

I'm outside in the garden.

I've been walking the same stretch of path, backwards and forwards, dozens of times, to and fro.

My head is still reeling.

The telephone calls from café booths that weren't answered. My suspicions, my imaginings. Had he actually been following me? From the station to the café to the hotel . . .

The shopping lists, had those just been the excuse he was offering me for my Wednesday afternoons between the crisp starched sheets? The Japanese paper, the canvas, the paints, the elusive and unattainable permanent violet?

Through the ripples and glissandos, through the running reflections on the surface of the water . . .

A face is upturned.

The mouth carries the bold semblance of a smile, all pearly white teeth. But the eyes are hollow, the sockets picked clean by the fish that dart in and out of the holes in the flesh, into the skeleton of bleaching bones, like the vaults and arches of a drowned cathedral.

'I'm okay, Ailsa.'

'Can you speak up a wee bit? The line's bad. It's hard to hear you –'

'I just said, I'm okay, thanks.'

'You don't sound terribly okay.'

'Well, I am. I assure you.'

'If you say so.'

'I do.'

'We'll probably be back in London the month after next. Ming's got a conference.'

'You're welcome to London.'

'Missed that, Eilidh. Say it again, will you?'

'I think my time here is accounted for. In Cassis.'

'That's a pity.'

'No, no. It's how I want it to be.'

'Oh, Eilidh!'

'I know my own mind.'

'Yes. I didn't say you –'

'I'm quite sure. About everything. I was never surer.'

'And you're staying on down there?'

'Yes. Yes, I am.'

'In that house?'

'Till it falls down. Or they carry me out.'

Laughter ricochets down the line at me. But I only meant to speak the blunt truth of the situation.

Colin Brogan's posthumous fame wasn't long in starting.

He was seen to be an 'existentialist artist', because he had been painting in France in the cultural slipstream of Sartre and Camus. The fact that he had maintained few contacts with Britain meant that his working methods were conveniently mysterious – they had an Olympian inaccessibility – all sorts of heavyweight philosophical claims could be made for him.

At the time there was need of a fresh young *intellectual* painter, and – dying so young, paragon of martyred 'jeunesse dorée' – he fitted the bill very nicely.

Academics took him up. They spoke of him as an internationalist, struggling with the ideals and realities of his age. The Riviera aspect was held to be tongue-in-cheek, following on from the earlier Scottish Colourists; he was subverting expectations about a publicity-hungry world in which the gossip-column names are revered in all their vacuous vulgarity. And where was closer to base for him than the David Niven–Jean Seberg milieu?

Et cetera.

* * *

First, they need to write to me.

I may or may not reply. If I reply and if I agree, I specify a date.

I wait for confirmation. I don't enter into negotiations about when.

On the day, at the appointed time, I expect to hear the tarnished brass bell jangling on the gate in the garden wall.

I walk down, at my own speed, and I ask who is there. I know who's due, the name of the person, and then I unbolt the gate, turn the key in the lock. I slowly pull back the gate, place myself in the narrowing angle of space behind, so that I can examine my visitor.

It's a little feat of gamesmanship. How to impose my own will on the situation. That's the surest part. It becomes less predictable later when they start to talk, when they get down to their probing and prying in the 45 or 60 minutes (never more) which I've granted them.

I answer their questions.

I'm required to think on my feet. I'm matched against wily professionals. They all want to serve themselves – using the name of Colin Brogan – for their own kudos and advancement, or for financial profit.

If I were to make one false step, they would be on to me. I need to be encouraging but reserved, cool and unflustered, shrewdly calculating, all at the same time.

It's acting, and I need to be a clever actress. No one is going to leave deflated, but I won't promise anything. With agreements, including their get-out clauses, if I nod my head and say 'yes' I make sure that I shall receive *my* due beforehand.

They know what to expect now, and would respect me less if I didn't drive a hard bargain. 'For the sake of my husband's reputation,' I tell them, and they say they understand.

I listen to her talking, this woman, and I watch her in the reflecting surfaces of the room as she leads another visitor where she has decided in advance to take them. She is polite, formal, and quite determined. I wonder where she's learned her skills, or if they are inherited in the genes.

* * *

I wrote to June McMurchie and asked if I might please read any other letters Colin had sent her.

There was nothing, I informed her, which I didn't know about our marriage. Nothing at all.

But for my own sake (I didn't tell her), I would be glad to have confirmation, to be able to put my mind at rest.

I don't tell Eilidh that I write – if she found out, she'd think I was betraying her – so these letters get sent either under cover of other letters, or because I say I have to buy stamps at the post office.

So, why do I involve **you**, June? Because if I didn't, I know I wd have to communicate my feelings somehow or other. I wd say something to Eilidh instead, blurt it out, & that wd be the start of the end, our life unravelling.

I tell her that I need some materials, from a couple of shops in the city centre. I have enough to last me of most things, but it gives her the excuse she needs. I give her the opportunity of a lie, so it's I who begin the process, I'm the one responsible, & so she's let off the hook.

I followed her today. To Marseille. To the cours Roosevelt, along the St-Savournin, the rue Terrusse, to the Hotel Madison. The closer I got, the more inevitable it seemed.

The hotel is like dozens of others, and so it's anonymous. Quite respectable, to all appearances. The clientele are reps, I imagine, travellers on a medium budget, which they'll fiddle, denying themselves a better hotel if it means they can pocket the difference.

L'Hôtel Duplicité.

But I can tell that he doesn't really give her happiness, or nothing that can last. Briefly he takes her out of herself, just long enough for her to realise there's no good point.

I feel only pity for her. Sorrow, compassion – what's the word? She mustn't have any inkling, though, because if I give myself away then **I'm** failing **her**, I'm the one who's defaulting.

I have to make my smiles easy & bright, inconsequential, the opposite of what I mean, like the reverse of pity.

*

He stops writing to his old friend. Either he hasn't the time any more, or he lacks the inclination: some matters have to remain private and undeclared.

* * *

I didn't return to Edinburgh. A couple of times I was nearly tempted, but I thought better of it. There was no need to see it again; the geography was there inside my head, fixed and constant – the New Town's streets and squares, the high pavements and back wynds.

It didn't concern me what Edinburgh was like now. I had delegated responsibility for my husband's reputation to a handful of appointees; we communicated by letter or by phone, and I couldn't see how anything would be gained by our meeting directly, face to face.

Morven had become her father's staunchest defender. She wouldn't hear any criticism of his abilities.

She had acquired several paintings which came up at auction, bidding over the odds for them. They were hung on her walls in Ainslie Place, not all of them prominently; some of the subjects were forgotten now, and – in the circumstances – would have loomed a little too presumptuously.

Ranald Guthrie's portraits suffered the commercial doldrums for several decades.

Now, even if not fashionable, they are admired for their draughtsmanship skills. Their attempts at image-making are considered by some quite advanced for the period, even if not 'ironic' enough for a modern audience.

But Ran Guthrie's prices have fallen a very long way behind the sums for which Colin Brogan's work sells.

The Guthries have a certain kitsch value, while

Brogan's main importance lies in his originality. Informed opinion has decided that the younger man had 'integrity', while Guthrie did not.

Ran Guthrie's life had finished in effect many years before, on the afternoon my mother died. All the succeeding time had been a kind of epilogue, lived out in half-colours. He had belonged to 'after' for such a long time that I really forgot he wasn't dead already.

Ailsa telegrammed to tell me that he had – in her words – 'passed on'.

I didn't reply. I lifted the receiver off the phone, and left it lying on the hall table.

I went up to the hotel on the Bestouan road, to the bar, to have the taste of a whisky and the distraction of the guests to watch.

I decided I would say I'd been away for a few days, I wasn't at home when the telegram came. I knew I couldn't go back to Edinburgh to face them at a funeral. It didn't matter to our father, and it wasn't going to affect the opinions which others had of me.

Only he and I, and my mother, had known the reason why I couldn't come.

* * *

They always ask me, what is *that* picture, eyes widening after they've spotted it at the back of the room.

I follow them, but at a distance. I pace my reply, and don't really tell them the half of it, only what I judge they need to know.

When I'm later asked to supply a written commentary on the paintings for a book, I choose my words carefully.

*

[THE DARK POOL]
He hung on to the painting, even when we really
couldn't afford to; selling it would have paid the rent for
a few weeks. He didn't want to let it go because it
summed up that watercolour time at Hourn, and his
learning to be quick and flexible.

Trees appear to be made out of metal, crippled by
their tension. The surface of water entangles them, pulls
them down into their reflections. Blue, from luminous
blue through midnight to pitch. A delirious dark roundel,
spun out of the tweed hills and bruised sky, the palette-
mess of streaked clouds.

I married him, but Colin Brogan still might have been a
stranger, with a separate life.

We were held together by dependence, because we served
one another, and by a kind of alchemy of ignorance, which
also served us.

We couldn't afford to know too much: he about my
history, and I about the methods of his imagination.

**In the latest study – does this signify a shift of critical
attitude? – Brogan has been criticised for not referring
to WW2 or to the Cold War or to technological
progress.**

He lived in his time, however, and he responded in his
own way. He painted out of every painting he'd seen in
his life, every book he'd read, every film he'd watched.
He had to consider every prejudice and heresy he was
capable of. But equally he wanted to create an idyll in
this troubling world, and he needed to find his own
personal vocabulary for it.

[UNTITLED]
Observed through an open door, I'm sitting up in bed,
hands cupping the bowl of coffee he's brought me. Head
a little bowed, I'm drinking thirstily, draining the big
white cup. I AM my thirst: no more and no less than the
sum of my simple instincts.

None of this Riviera is quite real. We wake to it every
morning. The blue sky, the sea like silk endlessly pulled over
rollers. The gassy heat hovering over rooftops, a haze of
white dust rising from a road in the distance.

Now, we're told, painters use the front part of their brain
to work, the area which deals with complex emotions.
The rest of us operate from the more systematic back
portion.
   A painter describes what he *feels*, not what he sees.

The road where the white dust blew took us by a long way
round to where we were heading all the time.
   First of all, there was Cassis.
   In the garden of 'La Croix du Sud' there's an almond
tree.

[ALMOND TREE]
The tree in our garden blazes into flower. The effect of
blossom on the branches is electric. A cascade of white
and blue energy. It hurts the eyes to look.

Years on, years later, these paintings will become very
well known. By that time Scotland will have reclaimed
him, and there will be a crying need for true talent to
celebrate. His paintings have the charge of the exotic
south, which marks them out from the voguish urban

[203]

realism and the hyped whizzkids using spurious philosophical titles to lend their work gravitas. Brogan's paintings show a way of life that's either desirable or sybaritic, according to taste, but more enduringly they have an enigmatic quality – who is the woman, what is the artist's relation to his subject, why these shadows and why the visible silence?

X is a figure shadowily asleep at a table while the burning almond tree is framed through a window, like something dreamed up but more actual than the dreamer, whose existence is the dreams inside her head.

CHAPTER TEN

Dusk

L unching alone as ever, Johnnie Melrose dropped down
dead in the Café Royal, over his crème caramel.

Ailsa sent me the *Scotsman* obituary. She said I mustn't tell
Morven, please. His dying didn't shock me, but the photograph did, having him here in the room with me.

The photograph was fifteen or twenty years old: an
illustration for a Melrose's catalogue perhaps. The man
was still in fine physical shape: seated in a chair, face
summer-tanned, fair hair combed and parted, fountain
pen in hand, the businessman's pose, but unable to resist
smiling at the camera. A slightly lopsided smile, pulled back
into his cheek, caught up over one incisor, brazenly wooing
the lens.

I couldn't sleep that first night after I'd received the news. I
had to get up and move about. I found the newspaper,
opened it out on the kitchen table at the page, walked round
and round the kitchen.

Three o'clock in the morning. They call it 'the hour of the
wolf' in the wilds of Italy.

The man is making his entrance into the room. I feel my
stomach flipping over, my skin goes clammy, my palms,
under my arms, the insides of my thighs.

I missed the green ray. I woke with my head down on the
old pine table, hearing birdsong in the garden.

I woke wondering, how often had he thought about me?

Or was it another of his unbreakable habits in later years, that he mustn't dare to remember?

I made coffee for myself. I took my cup outside. The garden felt washed clean after a dawn shower of rain. I didn't know why I wasn't feeling sadder, or sorer. Instead – inexplicably – I felt revived, and prepared for the business of another day ahead.

* * *

Nearly everything has disappeared into the past tense.

My husband. My mother. The father who raised me. Even the indestructible Johnnie Melrose in the end.

And, more recently, Morven's husband. The younger Rutherford also.

There's nothing to distinguish them now. They have all entered the kingdom of past things.

Soon this, too, will be 'was'. L'écossaise, the piano teacher. The house with green shutters. The overgrown garden.

The phrases of Debussy at odd times of the day and night. The slow footfalls on the gravel path. The rusty key turning in the lock of the old green gate and the stubborn bolt rammed shut once any callers have taken their leave.

Only the paintings aren't part of that process. They exist. They've rescued those moments of being and preserved them.

Insignificances (as I thought them) are granted a grandeur greater than tragedy and death.

I shall become 'was'. But also something of me will live on.

The past comes shining through everything. It shines from layers down, as if it's embedded in the paper or the canvas. It's as irrefutable to me as a watermark. It cannot be erased.

Proust understood the psyche of his painter, Elstir, perfectly well.
   Elstir, in order to find the enduring in his human subject-matter, had to (figuratively) destroy them first as individuals in a time and a place. Only then was he able to make a state-of-being permanent: youth, love, happiness, hopefulness. Life had to be sacrificed to make the art: the real yielded up the essence of itself, to have a life beyond itself.

Liver spots on the backs of my hands. The dancing brown flowers of death, falsely gay. But everything is leading *that* way. The primrose path. My mother spoke of her love of primroses, but they were the sort of flower people call their favourites without thinking, and I didn't believe her. Later at least I stopped believing her, when I looked back and considered that life, once it was over.
   Two Uffizi postcards which I long ago pinned to the kitchen wall.
   Mary Magdalene (attributed to Costa), contrite in a violet tunic as she kneels in prayer at Christ's feet.
   The Virgin Mary (by Aspertini), sorrowing beneath the bloodied Cross, face framed by the violet lining of her hood.

VIOLET   symbol of *humility*
             symbolises the love of truth and the truth of love,
                passion and suffering
             the colour traditionally worn by PENITENTS

Colin is staring up at me through the distance of water between us, with an expression of mild curiosity.

I'm looking down from my rock, unable to move.

I am nothing, no one. Can't he see that?

The effect, watching him, is the same as one of those aquarelles: shimmering depths, melting fields of vision.

The moments are everlasting. He is dancing a kind of ballet in the water beneath me, held in elegant metaphysical suspension. I am stuck to that rock, gazing down, mesmerised – spellbound – by what is happening.

Forgive me.

Forgive me my sins.

Forgive me, Colin, please.

* * *

Now it's dusk.

A garden in Cassis. Smoky blue shadows. Streaks of green and yellow in the sky. A big blood-orange sun sinking into the sea.

A dog barks somewhere. Cicadas trill. A motorbike putters up the road, goes over the brow of the hill.

A pine cone falls through the tree's branches, thumps on to the ground.

Stillness again, or what passes for stillness.

The same view I've looked at for nearly forty years. A tangle of trees, a cactus with one prickly arm raised, the stepped wall. A church tower, with red pantiles. Limestone cliffs. The little lighthouse at the end of the jetty.

Then the dog starts barking again. A guard dog somewhere, held by a chain, a grey dog as high as my waist with bright-yellow eyes: saucer-sized eyes, like the eyes of the dog in the story about the tinderbox, the story my mother might tell me once I was in bed, when she came in from wherever she'd been or before she was due to go out, anticipating a pleasurable evening.

It always comes back to that – Edinburgh. I'm a child again, and my mother is alive again. She is telling me a story to salve her conscience. Ran Guthrie has finished work in his studio, 'knocked off' on the dot of six, he's put down his paintbrushes and the distinguished sitter has left; the portrait remains propped on the easel; now he's home, I hear the front door close behind him, and then a couple of minutes later the top of a gin bottle rattles on to the silver salver.

Everything reaches its end.

As long as I had work to do, as long as my husband and his posthumous reputation needed me, there was a purpose to my life. While my pupils wanted to come to be taught, I welcomed them, but now I have arthritis in my finger joints. The garden has gone to seed, and the roof of the villa is letting in water, and every so often there's a rumour that the family of the original owner wants the property back.

My proper existence is in the paintings. By comparison, where I am and what I do and how I pass my days and nights – it all has little bearing.

There's a story to be told, and I am the only one who can tell it – even though in the process I have to show I was capable of much worse than the worst my detractors claim for me.

Colin Brogan is owed his life back again. And if I can't do that, I can say why he lost it, because at the time there didn't seem to be any other way, none at all.

Story told, then my usefulness will be over.

The house will return to shadows. The garden will become a wilderness. I won't be seen for several days, for a week. I'll have left the green gate propped open with stones, but inevitably the wind is too determined and it blows the gate shut. They will ring the bell on the wall, and my pupils and neighbours will debate the wisdom of breaking in before they finally do.

I am wherever I've chanced to fall.

I'm not breathing, and cold to touch.

Too late. She's dead. Dead and gone.

'*C'est fini!*' That's it.

On the kitchen table there's an old cardboard box, and inside the box a pile of pages covered with my handwriting. Someone picks up the top sheet, they start to read, and just where this manuscript ends the tale begins . . .

Acknowledgements

I referred to:

The Hogarth Book of Scottish Nursery Rhymes, collected
and edited by Norah and William Montgomerie (London: Hogarth Press, 1964).
George Ferguson, *Signs and Symbols in Christian Art* (New
York: Oxford University Press, 1954).

The Scottish Arts Council generously awarded a travel
grant to aid my background research in France.

Cover Photograph by Jacques-Henri Lartigue.